THE CATACOMBS

Cult #2

PENELOPE SKY

Hartwick Publishing

Hartwick Publishing

The Catacombs

Copyright © 2021 by Penelope Sky

All rights reserved.

No part of this book may be reproduced in any form or by any electronic or mechanical means, including information storage and retrieval systems, without written permission from the author, except for the use of brief quotations in a book review.

Contents

1. Constance — 1
2. Benton — 13
3. Constance — 35
4. Benton — 51
5. Constance — 65
6. Benton — 71
7. Constance — 75
8. Benton — 85
9. Constance — 103
10. Benton — 113
11. Constance — 127
12. Benton — 141
13. Constance — 153
14. Benton — 163
15. Constance — 173
16. Benton — 181
17. Constance — 201
18. Benton — 215
19. Constance — 225
20. Benton — 229
21. Constance — 241
22. Benton — 251
23. Benton — 263
24. Constance — 273
25. Benton — 281
    Epilogue — 291

    New From This Author… — 295

ONE

Constance

THE BUTTER SIZZLED AS THE PANCAKES COOKED IN THE pan, a dusting of cinnamon across each one, my little addition to the recipe. When raindrops the size of golf balls struck the windowpane, I jumped nearly a foot into the air. My eyes squeezed tightly together, and I released a painful sigh.

"Is breakfast ready?" Claire's sweet voice came from behind me, a ray of sunshine in this rainstorm.

"Almost." My eyes glanced at the clock on the microwave, hoping that Benton would walk through the door any minute.

Claire climbed onto the chair at the dining table and sipped her orange juice.

"Should we drive today?" I scooped the pancakes out of the pan and onto the plate.

"I like the rain."

I chuckled. "Of course you do." Just when I turned

around with the food, the front door opened. I stopped in my tracks at the sound, my heart in my throat, a tremor in my hand. The relief wouldn't dissolve into my blood until I heard his voice or saw his face.

His heavy footsteps grew louder as he moved all the way down the hallway. Then he emerged a moment later, in a gray long-sleeved shirt and black jeans, his blue eyes tired from a long night doing…whatever he did. They locked on to mine, reading my expression like subtitles on a TV screen.

The breath left my lungs, removed the anxiety, and then my entire body relaxed.

He was home.

His eyes settled on me for a while, as if he knew every single thought as it streaked across my mind, even before he rounded the corner.

I made it the rest of the way and set the platter on the table.

Claire grabbed a pancake with her bare hand and took a bite. "Constance and I are going to walk in the rain."

He came to her and kissed her on the head. "Don't want you to get sick, sweetheart."

"I don't care."

He gave her a quick rub on the head before he walked into the kitchen and made himself a cup of coffee. Even if he was tired and ready for bed, he couldn't resist a hot cup of coffee with his breakfast. He took a seat next to Claire across from me and ate his pancakes and roasted potatoes.

The slightest sound nearly gave me a heart attack. All night, I listened for the door, waiting for Benton to come home, afraid it would be someone else. Once upon a time, I had been a different person. Carefree. Easygoing. Unafraid. But now I was a scared chickenshit…and I hated it. The only time I could enjoy being alive was when this man was here.

He stared at me as he ate, elbows on the table, his hair slightly damp from being in the elements. The stare had been intimidating at one point, but now it brought me the most comfort. He was the only person in the world who could stare at me like that and not receive a snide remark as a consequence.

"Want to come with us?"

He put a bite of food into his mouth, chewed, and gave a slight nod in response.

I tried not to appear so desperate for his companionship, but it was inevitable. I felt the held breath slowly leave my lungs.

"Daddy, can we walk?"

His stare was so focused on my face that he didn't hear the question. His thoughts consumed him, drowned him so deep under the surface that he tuned out everything around him.

Claire was all that mattered to him. So…what could make him forget her, even just for a split second?

He would probably never tell me—even if I asked.

BENTON PUT the vehicle in park at the drop-off line and walked around the front in the pouring rain to get Claire out of the back. He opened her pink umbrella then held it out to her so she could be covered from the heavy raindrops. He helped her get her backpack on, gave her a kiss, and then said goodbye. "Have a good day, sweetheart."

"Bye, Daddy." She walked to the building, purposely splashing in the puddles with her boots.

Benton got back into the car and took off before the parent behind him could honk their horn. We were back on the road, the tires splashing the pools of rain along the way. Few people were on the sidewalk, and the ones who were all held large umbrellas over their heads.

I'd never been in the company of someone where silence was the preferred choice of communication. He hardly said anything, and I never felt responsible for filling the awkward quiet because it wasn't awkward at all.

The music was off. He drove with one hand on the wheel. As if I wasn't there, he lived in his own world.

"Christmas is coming up…"

He gave me a side look.

"Do you guys do anything special for the holiday?"

His eyes returned to the road, and he pulled up to a stoplight. He hit the blinker, ready to turn left once the light turned green. "No."

"No tree or anything?"

"Yes, there's a tree. And gifts from Santa."

"You do the Santa thing?" I asked, slightly surprised he would allow a fictitious fairy tale inside the household.

"Yes." He turned to give me a look, as if he dared me to make a jab.

"That's cute."

He looked forward again, his eyes reflecting the red light.

"Claire goes on Christmas break soon, so should I get a tree?"

"You'll never be able to do that by yourself."

"I'm a lot more capable than you think."

The light turned green, and he made the turn, pulling onto our street. "We'll go together when Claire gets home. She likes to pick out the tree."

"Oh, that's great."

He pulled up to the back of his apartment and tucked his Range Rover into the garage. We entered the apartment, shielded from the pouring rain, the heated floors making it the coziest place I'd ever been.

His shoulders were drenched with water spots because he'd exposed himself to the rain, his hair a little flat because it was damp too. But he never seemed to mind physical discomfort. Whether it was going outside nearly naked and barefoot in the freezing cold to look for an intruder or helping his daughter in the pouring rain. "I'm going to bed."

"How was last night?"

He stilled at the question, his eyes piercing my face like small daggers.

"I'm not prying. Just…want to know how things are going."

He never gave an answer before he walked down the hallway to his bedroom.

"Benton?"

He stilled without turning around, his enormous mass blocking out most of the hallway. He turned his body slightly but never turned around entirely. The side of his face was visible, his jawline hard, his neck thick with veins.

"I didn't sleep well last night…"

His head finally turned my way, his stare fixed on me, and he gave a subtle nod in the direction of his bedroom.

THE RAIN NEVER LET UP.

I slept for hours by his side, and when I woke up, the rain was still loud against the windows, even audible against the roof on the second story, a floor above us. My clothes were on the floor, and I was in my underwear beside him. Nothing physical happened because he seemed more interested in sleep than sex.

I was wide awake now, but the house didn't require my attention. Leftovers were on the menu for dinner tonight, and the laundry was done. There was nowhere else for me to be, so I lingered, comfortable in the warm sheets, safe with this man beside me.

When he was asleep, his face was different. The sternness of his jawline was altered, relaxed. His shoulders weren't so rigid, and he wasn't tense in preparation for a provocation. He was at his kindest.

Hours later, he grew restless, his large mass changing positions more often. He turned on his side and came closer to me, his arm instinctively reaching out and landing around my waist.

I didn't mind.

Our heads were close together now, on the same pillow, his manly smell right in my face.

I studied his hard cheekbones, his chiseled jawline, his massive shoulders that poked out from underneath the sheets.

It was hard to believe he was the same man from the theatre, that our relationship started there and ended up here. We were both touched by the camp—just in very different ways.

His sleepy eyes opened and immediately focused on my face. It seemed to take a few seconds for him to digest his sight. A deep breath was pulled into his lungs, and his arm slowly withdrew, his hand stopping at my hip.

The rain continued to pour, louder than it'd ever been. The thunder started, far away at first, but almost deafening as it drew near. The natural sounds of the apartment no longer disturbed me. I didn't jolt when the heater kicked on, when the floorboards creaked from the change in temperature, when Claire's open door shut once the air pushed it closed. This man gave me peace—and I was addicted.

After a long stare, he turned over and reached into his nightstand.

I pushed off my panties and left them on the sheets at my feet.

After he was ready to go, he rolled back over, his massive body getting on top of mine, one arm hooked behind a knee. There was no preamble, not even a kiss. He was inside me with a thrust and a moan, and then his massive body worked me and the mattress to make his headboard tap against the wall at the pace of a galloping horse.

I clung to him and enjoyed it, nails digging into his hard flesh, moaning against his jawline. It was so damn good, the union between our bodies, the inherent security it provided. It was an ascension, but one I actually enjoyed.

He didn't give a damn about anyone or anything, but he always made sure I got my fix before he had his. He made sure my toes curled until they cramped, made sure my body tightened around him so hard it must have hurt. He gave me every reason to draw blood with my nails, as if he liked the pain.

He finished, his hard eyes on mine, his handsome face slightly flushed with arousal. The tense muscles started to relax, and he withdrew and cleaned off. His heavy body returned to the mattress beside me, one arm behind his head, his eyes turned toward the curtain-covered window where it continued to pour.

I rolled onto my side, so relaxed that I never wanted this moment to end. The stress was gone from the very insides of my muscles, from the lining of all my organs, from every place where it was tucked.

It was as if Hell had never happened.

He grabbed his phone from the nightstand and scrolled through his messages before he hit the button and returned the screen to darkness. He was bare-chested with the sheets around his waist, his hard body concrete with lines carved by the edge of a knife. He lay there, his eyes on the ceiling. "I assumed the rain would be gone by now."

"We'll get the tree tomorrow. I can do your shopping for you if you give me a list of what you want."

"She's hard to shop for—because I buy her whatever she wants."

"I noticed." I gave a smile as I pulled the sheets farther up my shoulder. "Never seen a little girl with so many stuffed ponies…and real ponies."

His eyes turned to the window. "Before she was born, I told myself I wouldn't spoil her. I would discipline her. I wouldn't let her believe in princesses and Prince Charming and all that bullshit that doesn't exist."

"I believe in those things…"

"How?" His head turned to me, his eyes hard. "You've seen the real world. The nightmares. The monsters. The evil."

"Well, Claire feels like a real princess to me."

His hard eyes instantly released.

"And you're her Prince Charming who came to save her."

He looked at the ceiling again.

"So yes, I still believe in that stuff."

He had closed off entirely, invisible walls all around his mind and body.

"Are your parents still around?" I asked.

"No."

"I'm sorry."

His open eyes stared, focused on the ceiling like it was more than just a simple wall.

"How was your night last night?"

"You already asked me that."

"I thought you were just too tired to answer."

"No."

"I'm not trying to pry—"

"I don't do pillow talk, alright?" He propped himself up on his elbow as he rolled over and looked down at me, his gaze fierce. "You want to fuck me to make yourself feel better? That's fine with me. But I'm not doing all the other shit that comes along with it. Got it?"

I stilled at the outburst, the calm haze shattered.

He threw the sheets off then sat upright, his legs over the edge, his strong back to me. He inhaled a slow and deep breath, his eyes on the window hidden behind the closed curtains. A nearly empty glass with a drop of scotch was on his nightstand, along with a gun that he had pulled out of the back of his jeans when he stepped inside.

"It's not pillow talk, Benton." I sat up, my body against the headboard, my naked skin cold the moment he was gone. "It's called friendship…but you obviously don't know what that is."

TWO

Benton
———————

"Dad, I like this one." The horrid rain had finally come to an end, but the streets and pavement still reflected the lampposts like mirrors. Claire's pink rain boots hit a puddle, and she splashed right through on the way to the tree that caught her eye.

I looked it up and down, its short stature, its dying branches that were turning brown and bald at the ends. It was offered at half the price—which was still too expensive for this piece of shit.

Constance walked over, in a gray pea coat with a gold necklace, her arms folded over her chest, black gloves on her fingers. She looked at Claire and gave a slight chuckle. "It's…nice."

It was a dead tree with a price tag. "Pick another one, Claire."

"But I want this one—"

"No." I flashed my stare on her, telling her not to argue with me in a public setting. I'd rarely had to spank her as a child, and it only happened a few times for the obedience to settle in. She was too old for that now, but time-outs were still on the table.

She kicked a rock before she moved to the next tree.

Constance watched her go before she turned her stare on me. Green eyes full of intelligence speared me. She never regarded me with a look of longing like the others, like she wanted to sink her claws into my flesh and attach me to her permanently. It was a different look entirely. Couldn't explain it.

After the contact had lasted a while, she followed Claire. "This one's beautiful. I love the smell of pine needles this time of year."

"Yeah…" Claire tugged on one of the branches and watched it bounce, drops of water spraying everywhere. "Let's get this one."

"Whatever…"

Constance stood beside her, her hands in the pockets of her jacket. "Why do you want the other tree?"

"Because no one else is going to buy it."

My daughter had a big heart, would take any charity case that showed up on our doorstep. Anytime we saw a stray animal, she wanted to keep it, but I was in no position to raise my daughter and take care of a pet, so I had to find them homes and listen to her cry every time I gave them away.

Constance turned her head to watch Claire. "But if we don't get this tree, someone else might not choose it either."

Claire gave a shrug. "I just feel bad for him."

Constance gave a smile before placing her arms around my daughter's shoulders, a look in her eyes that was completely genuine. The affection was real. The love unquestioned. I couldn't remember a time when Beatrice wore a look remotely similar. "Baby, that's so sweet." She rubbed her arms as she hugged her close. "How about this? We get this beautiful Douglas fir to put in the living room by the fire, and we get the other one to put in your bedroom?"

When Claire looked up at her, there were fireworks in her eyes. "Really?"

"It'll be my Christmas gift to you." She pulled her close and pressed a kiss to her forehead.

"Thanks, Constance." Claire gave her a squeeze then ran off to the emaciated tree that belonged in the chipper.

Constance watched her go before her eyes turned back to me. The smile faded. Her gaze hardened, as if she expected me to challenge her.

I didn't.

———

I CARRIED the bigger tree inside to the left of the fireplace. There were just a few inches from the top of the tree to the ceiling, enough room for Claire to hang up the star when we decorated.

The other was put in Claire's room near the door, pine needles dropping everywhere because the thing had been dead a while. It would only last a week before it was a skeleton of dead branches.

But Claire was happy, so it didn't matter.

"Can we decorate the tree now?" Claire asked.

"It's time for bed."

"*Pleeeaassse.*"

My eyes narrowed, and that was all I needed to do.

She dropped her head and headed off to bed.

"Tomorrow, sweetheart." After she brushed her teeth and put on her pajamas, I tucked her in for the night, the dead tree casting shadows that looked like long, lifeless fingers. I stroked her hair and gave her a kiss.

"Can we decorate this tree too?"

If we bought ornaments and lights, it would be a commitment. And that commitment would turn into a tradition. I'd have one of the ugliest trees on the lot in my home every single year.

But I couldn't say no. "Sure."

I turned off the light and shut the door. The night was over for the two of them, but mine was just getting started. I grabbed my gun from my nightstand and prepared to head out.

"You're leaving?" Constance was on the couch in the living room, her pea coat on the coatrack so she was in her blouse and tight jeans. Her dark hair perfectly fell around her face, soft and shiny.

The howls of the demon played in my mind, the deep baritone of his cries, the high-pitched level of his screams. The tantrum had been so unnatural that I would never forget it. The breaks in the syllables of his speech, the way his fingers curled into fists as if he were imagining her dress in his grasp.

Her stare continued, waiting for an answer.

With those fair cheeks and deep eyes, she was worthy of his obsession. Even dressed in all black as she was now, she was still angelic. Just her voice alone was ethereal, as if she belonged somewhere far above the earth. "Yes."

She left the couch and approached me in the foyer, the gold necklace around her throat casting a glimmer of reflection from the dimmers in the ceiling. She always called me out on my bullshit, but she never held a grudge either. It was forgotten the moment it happened. It reminded me of the way I was with Bleu, like the connection between us was stronger than anything that happened outside of it. It was elemental, unconditional, almost permanent. "I don't know what you're out there doing, but whatever it is, be careful."

My eyes shifted back and forth as I looked into her eyes, seeing a woman who relied on me the way a wife relied on her husband, who berated me the way a sister would her brother, overrode me the way a mother would override a father. "You never have to worry about me."

Her eyes dropped. "I know you don't give a shit about me, but I give a shit about you." Her eyelashes stretched over her cheeks as she looked down, some of her hair falling forward past her shoulders. She looked up again, not an ounce of self-pity in her gaze. She was matter-of-fact. Straight to the point. Uncomplicated.

"Why?"

The question moved into her eyes.

"Because of the sex? Or because of the roof over your head?"

Now her eyes narrowed and her brow took on an angry furrow. "I don't know what happened to you to make you like this...and I'm sorry that it happened... but I'm not the one who did it. I'm not the one who scarred you."

"Answer my question."

Her arms tightened over her chest, her head slightly cocked to the side. "I think that answer is obvious."

"Not to me."

She gave a subtle shake of her head, venomously disappointed. "Because of Claire. I love your daughter. I would die for her...literally. Why isn't that enough for you to stop being an asshole? To let me in—"

"Why do I have to let you in at all? You're the goddamn nanny—"

"I'm a hell of a lot more than that, and you know it." The anger turned to raw, burning pain. "The three of us have been to hell and back—literally. We keep going around and around with this over and over again, and I don't..." Her eyes dropped momentarily, as if a thought struck her right in the chest. When she looked at me again, I saw calm realization there, as if everything suddenly made sense. "I'm not just going to walk out on your daughter the way Beatrice did. I'm not going to abandon her. I'm not going to abandon you either."

I held her gaze, stony.

"This is home to me now."

The shrieking came back again, the screams louder than they were last time.

"So please, stop with the asshole thing. I care about you. You care about me. We're a team. I had to take care of her by myself in that camp, and it's nice to have someone take care of me now. I'm not ashamed to say that. I'm not ashamed to say that I need you to keep me sane. We're like this weird, twisted—"

"Family."

She turned silent, her breaths heavy. "Yes…a family."

I stared at her expression as my words sank in.

"We're bonded together for life. The three of us. I'm like Bartholomew, your right-hand man. But I'm a woman who likes to jump your bones sometimes. It's not complicated…so don't make it complicated."

My eyes scanned her face for more information than she revealed, but there was nothing there. I was just the crutch that kept her on her feet, the bulletproof vest strapped to her chest, the gun in her hand. I was the fire in the snowstorm. I was the lone cabin in the woods. Nothing more. "Alright."

―――

BARTHOLOMEW SAT in the back seat beside me, the glow of his phone illuminating up his face with a blue light. One elbow was propped against the window, his closed knuckles against his temple.

The gunfire was audible, the shootout hot and fast. It lasted for a minute, maybe two. But then the last shot was fired, and silence ensued.

Bartholomew typed on his phone as if he didn't notice—or care.

I looked out my tinted window to the dark street, the glow of the Eiffel Tower far away in the distance.

Bartholomew slid his phone into his pocket and opened the door.

I took that as my cue and hopped out with him.

We walked together, both in jackets and boots, the pavement wet from the rain that hadn't let up this season.

"I wonder who made it."

He gave a shrug as he pulled his gun out of his pocket. He cocked it before carrying it at his side. "We're about to find out."

We crossed the pavement and moved through the hole in the fence before we approached the warehouse. Bodies of fallen men were scattered everywhere, rifles and handguns at their sides.

Our men were the victors—and they went around to grab all the ammunition.

We walked up to the locked doors, where they were already cutting through the bolt with a blowtorch.

Side by side, we waited. Bartholomew stuck his gun

into the back of his jeans again before he hung his arms by his sides. His eyes scanned the area as he gave a sigh of boredom. "So." He turned to me. "Had a change of heart yet?"

I met his gaze, my look cold.

He looked forward again. "That's a no."

I checked the bolt on the door. They were only halfway through.

"What did she say when you told her?"

Silence.

I felt his stare on the side of my face.

"You didn't tell her."

"She doesn't need to know—"

"Because you think she'll turn herself over to protect Claire."

I turned to meet his gaze. "Her safety is my problem, not hers. She doesn't need to know."

His arms crossed over his chest. "I don't know…I think a heads-up would be nice."

"She's already scared enough as it is. I'm not throwing more wood on that fire."

The bolt finally came undone.

"Sounds like you like this woman." He motioned for them to open the large door. The men moved together and put their weight on the side, pushing it sideways, getting it to slowly reveal the darkness beyond.

I ignored what he said.

"You're fucking her, aren't you?"

I walked in first and found the switch to light up the place. Bulbs flickered on along the ceiling, revealing the never-ending line of storage crates. I went to the first one and removed the wooden lid to expose the rifles and ammunition inside, properly stored so a bump in the road wouldn't jolt the triggers. I took out the first one and examined it. Completely unmarked. No sign of ownership or make. "Jackpot." I returned it to the crate.

Bartholomew gestured to his men. "Soak the place." His hand reached into his pocket and withdrew a lighter. His thumb struck the button, making a little flame emerge. Like a child, he watched it with fascination.

"All this work…to destroy it all."

"Yep."

"We could sell it. Or keep it for ourselves."

"Both great options." He released the button and let the fire die out. "But I'm just in one of those moods." He turned back to me, his arms resting on the crates. "You know, where I want everyone to think I'm some crazy son of a bitch."

"People thought that long before you blew up your own ship."

He gave a smirk. "They did, didn't they?"

"So, what's the real reason?"

The dousing began. Gasoline was poured into every corner of the warehouse. Millions of dollars in illegal artillery were soaked in the gas that would light up this place brighter than the Eiffel Tower. "I'm about to teach you something, Benton." One arm rested on the crate as he turned to regard me, as if his arm were on the counter at a café while we both waited for our espressos. "How do you negotiate with someone when you don't know what they want? Shit, I don't even know what I want…most of the time."

―――

WHEN I WALKED in the door, I could still smell breakfast.

Pancakes. Potatoes. A toasted baguette she'd picked up from Le Grenier à Pain, the bakery where I told her to do my shopping. It was farther away than the ones right by my apartment, but it was the best.

But the apartment was silent, which meant Claire already left for school.

I'd missed it—again.

I didn't just feel self-loathing, but loathing for Bartholomew. I had been thrust back into the game, a game I didn't want to play anymore but was now obligated. It was more than obligation…closer to indentured servitude.

I left my jacket on the coatrack and headed straight to the kitchen. The food was lukewarm in the pans, but at least it wasn't cold from sitting in the fridge for an hour. I scooped everything onto my plate and skipped the coffee.

She was on the couch in front of the fire, her fingers absentmindedly playing with a gold pendant on a chain. She shifted it back and forth near her jawline, her eyes watching the flames in the hearth. A closed book was on her thigh.

I took a seat at the dining table and ate in silence.

She didn't look at me.

It was the same silent comfort that I shared with Bartholomew, where we could be in the same room for hours but feel no need to speak. The silence could float there between us, causing no tension, no discomfort.

When the food was gone, I left the dirty plate in the sink then grabbed the decanter of scotch in the living room. I poured myself a glass and took a deep drink.

As if she realized I was there for the first time, she turned to look at me, her fingers pausing on her necklace.

When the glass was empty, I wiped away the drops with the back of my hand.

She was always in her street clothes unless it was time for bed. Tight jeans and boots. Blouses that were flattering on her tits and slender waistline. Her long brown hair was always styled in some way, but whether it was curled or straight, it was soft, easy for my fingers to run through. Her most beautiful feature was probably her eyes—because they shone with intelligence.

"What is it?"

She rested the gold pendant against her bottom lip as her gaze shifted back to the fire. "Didn't sleep well, is all…"

Now I wondered if she really had seen that freak in the window. "Why?"

"Nightmare." She released the necklace and let it fall back into place as her arms crossed over her stomach. "I have them pretty often, but this time, I couldn't fall back asleep." Her eyes stayed on the fire, as if she didn't expect me to stick around.

I was dead tired and ready to sleep off the night I'd had, but I lingered, for reasons unknown. "You should drink."

She turned back to me, her eyes showing the question she didn't ask.

"That's why I always drink before bed."

"You have nightmares too?"

I lowered myself onto the couch beside her, my hands coming together between my knees. "Always."

"What are your nightmares about…if you don't mind me asking?"

The second I was this close to her, I could smell her perfume. It was some floral scent, something new because I didn't recognize it. Must have done some shopping while she picked up the groceries. "Before everything that happened with Claire, it was always someone from my past coming back to haunt me." I couldn't say the details, not out loud. Not even think them. "By hurting Claire…" I cleared my throat and brushed it off. "But now, my little girl in angel wings… surrounded by those freaks…crying for her father to come save her."

Her hand instantly went to my back, stroking across my shoulders then down my spine. "What do you do?"

"The drunker I am, the easier it is to go back to sleep and forget it ever happened." I grabbed the decanter, refilled my glass, and then handed it to her. "Therapy. Drugs. None of it is as effective as a bottle."

She looked down into the glass before she took a sip.

I got to my feet and headed to the hallway. "You'll have to drink more than that for it to work."

A CHRISTMAS MOVIE was on the TV, and the small speaker on the entertainment center blasted a playlist of popular Christmas songs. The once-bare tree was now covered with white lights that wrapped all the way around, starting at the base then moving to the top. Claire picked an ornament then found a place to hang it on the tree.

I dug inside the box until I found my favorite.

It was a picture of the two of us when she was five. She'd wanted to ride horses since she could talk, so I'd put her on a saddle and held her in place on one of our horses at our home in the countryside. The picture had been on my nightstand ever since—until she stole it and took it to school to turn it into an ornament. Now it hung inside a papier-mâché wreath that she made. I used to like looking at it every single day in my bedroom, but now I looked forward to pulling it out of the box this time every year.

Constance must have noticed because she took the seat beside me and looked at the ornament. "Aww, that's a cute picture." Her hand instinctively went to my wrist, her touch warm, a bit affectionate. When she realized what she was doing, she retracted her hand. "Where are you going to hang it?"

"Daddy, right here." Claire pointed at the bottom, where it would hang a couple inches off the floor.

"How about here, sweetheart?" I walked up to the tree and hung it higher, at my shoulder.

"Yeah, I guess that's okay." Claire went to the box to grab another ornament.

Constance gave a chuckle. "I can see who runs the show around here."

I hung the ornament in place then watched Claire move to the platform I'd built for her. I'd always been aware of my surroundings, but after I became a father, that focus deepened to an extraordinary level. Her foot moved to the step, but it was just her toes, so before she could fall, I caught her. My hand grabbed her by the arm and pulled her up so she wouldn't slip.

It all happened so quickly that she didn't even notice. She rose on her tiptoes so she could hang the ornament as high as possible. "How's that?"

"Very nice, sweetheart."

She stepped down and retrieved another ornament.

Constance watched us with a mug of hot cocoa in her hands, marshmallows floating on top. There was a brightness in her eyes I hadn't seen in a long time, like spending the holiday season with my daughter truly brought her joy.

Why didn't it ever bring Beatrice joy?

Claire carried a reindeer ornament to Constance. "Want to hang it up?"

"Honey, that's so sweet." Constance gave her a one-armed hug and rubbed her back. "But you and your dad should do this together. I'm happy to watch."

"Come on." I gave a nod toward the tree.

Constance switched her gaze to me.

"There's a good spot right here." I pointed to an opening between various ornaments.

Claire tugged on her arm. "Yeah!"

Constance moved her mug away, expertly preventing a spill as if she'd been taking care of a child as long as I had. "Alright." She took the ornament then came to me, examining the reindeer as it spun on the hook. "Here?"

I nodded.

She rose on her tiptoes and raised her arms in the air, the curve in her back deepening in the process.

I glanced instinctively, but I forced my gaze away since my daughter was right there.

Constance stepped back and admired her work. "Looks great."

"We've got more." Claire returned to the box of ornaments to fetch another one.

Constance continued to admire the lone ornament, her bright eyes reflecting the white lights that shone back at her. Her arms crossed over her chest and her stare remained, as if her mind had wandered elsewhere.

Claire came to her side with another ornament. "Hang this one up."

Constance smiled as she took it from her. "I'm on it."

Blanketed by the Christmas music, the warm fire,

the hot cocoa, it was easy to forget the rain outside, forget that the world outside these walls was a terrible place, full of demons and criminals.

The box started to become empty, so I took a seat on the couch and let the girls finish what was left since they were having a good time. Constance was picky about the spots she chose, and she always stopped to consider her next move. Claire was a torpedo, zooming back and forth like it was a race to decorate the tree.

But then she stopped.

She stood at the coffee table where the box sat, looking inside as if she saw something that perplexed her. Her hand reached inside and withdrew a statue of an angel. It was white ceramic and smooth.

For the first time in my life, I was paralyzed.

Constance seemed to pick up on the tension because she turned around and stilled when she saw the item in Claire's hand.

Claire dropped it back into the box and continued to stare down at it.

Constance immediately turned to me, her eyes giving that same sheer panic she'd shown me many times in the past.

The paralysis passed, and I sprang into action. "We don't need to keep it." It took all my willpower to sound normal, to keep my voice gentle, to force all the rage out of my tone. I grabbed the ornament and marched outside. I stepped outside the front door, down the stairs of my stoop, and into the pouring rain. My shirt was instantly soaked down to my skin, waterdrops rolling down the bridge of my nose like a stream. I squeezed the statue then slammed it down onto the sidewalk. It smashed into hundreds of tiny pieces, a pile of shards. There was no way to know what it had been before because it was mutilated beyond recognition. I looked up and down the street then walked back inside.

———

CLAIRE WAS TUCKED into bed with her stuffed hippo in her arms. With the sheets to her shoulder and her eyes closed, she looked as peaceful as ever.

But I knew there was more underneath.

My fingers combed through her blond hair, coaxing her into her dreams. A love like this was indescribable. Every fear she felt, I felt it a million times worse. Every pain, every sorrow, was as much of a burden to me as it was to her.

I had the power to do a lot of things, but I couldn't change the past.

I'd give anything to erase what happened. To erase everything she'd seen.

"Daddy?"

My hand stilled because I thought she'd been asleep. "What is it, sweetheart?"

"I didn't mean to make you sad…" Her eyes opened to meet mine. "Whenever it comes up, you get really sad."

All I could do was inhale a deep breath, the kind that hurt your lungs because you sucked in too much. I wanted to lie to her sweet little face and pretend everything was just fine, but she wasn't fine and neither was I. "I just missed you so much while you were gone."

"I know."

"If you ever need to talk about it…" My eyes flicked away because I couldn't be her priest. I couldn't be her therapist. It was just too hard for me, to listen to her describe the things they tried to do to her. The only reason it hadn't come to pass was because of the woman down the hall, the woman who saved us both. "We can find someone for you."

"I like to talk to Constance."

I gave a nod in encouragement, doing my best to keep a straight face and not let the breaths turn to sobs. "That's a good idea, sweetheart." I leaned over and gave her a kiss on the forehead. "Goodnight. I love you."

"Daddy?"

I just wanted to leave. I just wanted to hide my face. But I held on. "Yes, sweetheart?"

"There were still women there when I left… What happened to them?"

"They got home safe." I'd never had to lie to anyone until I became a father. I didn't care how much the truth hurt. If someone didn't want the hard truth, I was the wrong person to ask, because I would deliver it on a silver platter. But with Claire…I buried her fears with my lies. "Don't worry about them."

"Good."

I gave her a pat on the arm before I left her

bedroom. I shut the door behind me, and the second I heard it click into place, I closed my eyes. An avalanche of emotions hit me, forcing my chest to gasp for air, for my eyes to smart despite how tightly I shut them. My hand was still on the doorknob, but I wished it were a gun—and Forneus was at the end of it.

A hand moved to my arm, the touch delicate. Fresh-cut flowers on a summer day entered my nose. The fingers moved up my arm, to my shoulder, and then cupped my neck.

As if she issued the command with her words, I opened my eyes and met hers.

Her expression was identical to mine…in every way.

The toll made her eyes glisten with unshed tears. Her eyes weren't shallow and superficial like most people's. They were deep and cavernous, like there was no bottom to their depths. They went all the way to her heart, which was shattered into pieces like mine. As her hand cupped my neck, she moved closer to me, the connection between our eyes raw and infinite. Her other hand found its way to my bicep as she cradled herself closer to me.

Farther and farther, she inched, our faces so close together.

She dropped her head slightly, her forehead pressing against my lips as her arms circled me. Before I knew what was happening, she embraced me, our chests together, her body cocooned in mine.

My mind didn't override my body this time, and my arms circled her waist as I brought her close. My chin rested on her forehead, and I got a deeper inhale of her smell. The other times our bodies had been in contact with each other, it was mixed with heat and sweat. In the hallway outside my daughter's bedroom, I held her as she held me, the only person in the world who truly understood my pain.

Not just understood it—but shared it.

THREE

Constance

I walked Claire to school the next morning, and she was quiet.

That was unlike her. She usually splashed in the puddles with her rain boots, pointed at the clouds and said they looked like frogs and sharks, and asked me questions about everything that came to mind.

But now, her head was down, her hands on the straps of her backpack.

"You doing okay, honey?"

She kept her eyes on the sidewalk as she continued forward. "I'm fine."

"You're awfully quiet."

She gave a shrug.

I tried to cheer her up. "What if we get some gelato when I pick you up later?"

"Yeah?" That got her to look up, some light in her eyes. "That'd be fun. Will Daddy come?"

"I'm sure." After I dropped her off at school, I

stopped by the bakery Benton liked and picked up his usual list of items. I went to the store every other day because he liked his food fresh, so nothing lasted long. All the items on his list were things that belonged in the fridge, not the cabinets or the freezer. Cooking had never been my strong suit, as Claire had pointed out on multiple occasions, but I was rising to the challenge.

Juggling all the bags, I made it home and put everything on the counter. The house was quiet with Claire gone. Benton must still be asleep in his bedroom. I put everything away and noticed that the leftovers in the pan were gone.

Then I heard his voice. "I don't have time for this shit. Just get it done."

Once everything was put away, I made my way to the second floor where his voice came from. I hardly ever went up there. It had Beatrice's old bedroom, his weight room, and a study. I made my way down the hallway then took a peek inside.

Shirtless, he sat at a large desk. His chair was pivoted toward the window, and with one elbow on the desk, he stared through the part in the curtains, the overcast light blanketing his face. He must have just showered because his jaw was cleanly shaved, and his hair was flat as if it was still damp.

I would normally speak the moment I spotted him, but I chose to stay quiet and stare.

Blanketed in the morning light, the veins down his arms were pronounced, like thick ropes that secured ships to a dock. His skin was tight over his bulky muscles, so the outline of each one was distinct. He must lift trucks to look like that. His only soft feature was his eyes—which were still pretty hard.

It was difficult not to stare. Devoid of emotion for everyone except his daughter, he was one of the most heartless men I'd ever met, but he somehow made my heart full. I'd never felt such affection for any man in all my life. He was the light in the storm. The umbrella in the rain. The summer after the winter.

"Yes?" His deep voice had a rumble to it, like the bass from the speakers in the car. He didn't even glance at me but seemed to know I was there. Seemed to feel me. Seemed aware of his surroundings at all times—even when he was deep in thought.

I stepped farther into his study, seeing a large desk with a laptop and some papers. There was also a picture of Claire there, a school portrait, probably taken last year. Her hair was a lot shorter in the picture. "How are you?"

He kept his eyes on the window.

"Want me to pick you up an espresso—"

"You take care of my daughter—not me." He turned in his chair, pulling his eyes off the window and putting them on me. "And I hate that question."

"Why?"

"Because my answer is always the same." His wide chest was powerful, covering the entire chair behind him. Each of his pecs was the size of a steering wheel. His greatest strength was his stare—the intensity could move mountains.

"Are you home for the day?"

"Yes."

I felt the kick in my stomach, the overwhelming relief. "I told Claire I would take her out for ice cream after school if you'd like to join us."

His stare continued.

"But if you have other things to do—"

"How was she this morning?"

I gave a shrug. "Quiet."

He dropped his gaze, like a knife had plunged into his heart.

"She'll be okay, Benton."

He stared at his desk for a while before his hand rubbed his head, ruffling his hair. "The cut isn't what kills you. It's what happens afterward—when you bleed to death or die from an infection. She seemed well, but maybe I just pretended she was for my own sake."

"I think she is well. It just reminded me…that's all."

He looked away. "Every time she sees an angel, she's going to go through this."

"That can happen with anything. If you got bit by a dog, you'd be scared of dogs. If you got hit by a car, you'd be scared to drive. It's just a part of life. Doesn't mean there's something deeply wrong with her."

He kept his eyes on the window.

"I know you're worried, but she's strong."

His eyes flicked back to me.

"Like her father."

WHEN I FINISHED PREPARING LUNCH, he came downstairs and sat at the dining table. Still in just his sweatpants, he never bothered to get dressed—not that I minded. Somehow, his nakedness made me feel more secure because I knew he didn't need a weapon when he was a weapon himself.

I sat across from him and watched him dig into his food. With his arms on the table, he inhaled his meal, scarfing everything down as if he'd skipped breakfast that morning. His eyes were down most of the time, like I wasn't even there.

I took my time with my food because I couldn't just eat however much I wanted and stay trim.

He took a bite and chewed, his eyes lifting to meet my face.

There had never been much activity in my personal life. I worked a lot of nights at the theatre, so I didn't have a lot of opportunities to go out and meet someone. I hooked up with a couple dancers, but those were short-lived flings. Relationships were rare, and if they did happen, they were short. Never even came close to living with a man. But now I shared my life with the man across from me.

And I couldn't imagine being anywhere else.

Even if Forneus weren't lurking in the shadows, it would be impossible to go back to a normal life as if nothing had happened. I'd probably have to move like Beatrice. Start over somewhere new, somewhere that wouldn't remind me of all the horrors I'd witnessed. But even if I did that…I would never be okay.

Benton was the only thing that made me feel okay. Now his eyes didn't leave my face. "What is it?"

"What is what?"

"I can read your eyes."

I'd never been with a man in tune with my emotions, who could read my moods and thoughts like he felt them pressed directly against his skin. Was he just good at that sort of thing? Or was it because of what we had together? "I just… I don't know what I would do without you." My eyes dropped before I finished talking because I regretted what I said before I even said it. The first time I'd seen him was in the theatre, desperately asking everyone about Claire. He was just a stranger then. It was hard to believe he'd ever been a stranger. Our lives were tied together so tightly that it seemed impossible we'd ever lived separately.

The silence reigned, along with the heaviness.

I kept my eyes on my food, still unable to look up and see his reaction. He was probably annoyed…just like he was with everything else. I had the strength to kill a Malevolent, to stand up to Forneus, to tape those papers on the windows of the church. But it took a lot more strength to raise my chin and meet his gaze.

Still as a gargoyle, blue eyes carved in stone, he stared. "I know what I would do without you. I'd be here alone—without my daughter."

I RINSED the dishes in the sink, my eyes down on my work. They moved from right to left, the clean dishes sitting in the bottom of the other sink so they could be placed into the dishwasher when I was done.

My hand released the button on the nozzle when I felt him behind me.

His chest was against my back.

Both hands gripped the counter on either side of me, boxing me in.

The sharp breath I took was so deep it hurt, especially when I held it immediately afterward.

His mouth dipped to my neck, placing a kiss so soft that his hard mouth was hardly recognizable. His lips moved closer to my shoulder, his kisses growing more aggressive as he went.

My eyes closed, and I breathed again.

His powerful arms locked around me, one across my chest with his hand clamped on my shoulder. The other slid underneath my shirt and across my stomach, his hand reaching all the way around me to my back. He tugged me hard against him as he kissed my neck again, this time devouring me.

My hand reached behind me to cup the back of his neck. I tugged on him as I rolled my head back over his shoulder, exposing myself so he could take all of me. "Yes…" Every touch of his lips was morphine to my aching body. Every touch of his hands was lidocaine to my muscles. I spun in his arms, circled my arms around his neck, and kissed him like it was the first time all over again.

Our mouths moved together in perfect harmony, his breaths filling my lungs at the perfect time. His lips were full and soft, and he used them with the same purpose as he did with everything else. My fingers dug into his short hair as I was swept off my feet, to the safest place I'd ever known—his embrace.

As if I weighed nothing at all, he lifted me into him and carried me down the hallway to his bedroom. One large hand supported my ass, while the other remained in my hair, keeping it out of my face as he devoured my mouth.

My back hit the mattress when he dropped me. He kneeled in front of me and yanked off both boots before he moved up and pulled off my jeans and panties in a single tug. His bedroom eyes weren't much different from his normal stare because he was so innately sexy, but they were a little harder now than before—like he wanted me as much as I wanted him.

I pulled my blouse over my head then unclasped my bra, getting naked on top of his bed.

He dropped his bottoms and revealed his massive cock. Thick. Long. Carved out of marble by an artist. Six foot something with narrow hips and massive shoulders, he was a statue himself, a Roman emperor who conquered everything in his path. A thick vein from the base of his dick up his pelvis toward his stomach because he was so tight everywhere. A prominent V was distinct over his hips. The lines of his abs were so dark, it looked like permanent marker. He seemed to take his time, to let me enjoy the sight of his body before he moved for his nightstand.

I blurted out the words like I had at the dining table. "I have an IUD…"

He stilled at the statement, his blue eyes moving back to my face.

"I want to feel you…"

He regarded me for several seconds, his hard expression impossible to decipher.

I didn't want a barrier between us. I wanted that high to go even higher. I wanted that connection to be deeper. Swept up in the adrenaline and the desire, I was taken to a new plane of existence, a place where angels and demons didn't exist.

When he moved to the bed, that was my answer.

My legs opened, and I pulled him against me, getting his narrow hips perfectly between my thighs. My ankles hooked together around his waist, my heels grinding against his ass. One arm circled his neck, while my other hand planted against his chest, feeling the slow and steady beat of his heart.

He pushed inside me and sank.

"Oh…yes." My head rolled back as I gave a moan, feeling his bare skin under my fingertips, the hardness of his muscles, the heat of his skin. My eyes closed as the moment swept through me. When we were combined, it was a controlled fire, a desire that burned between us both without torching everything around us. It was just ours.

His heavy body started to rock, smothering me

against the mattress, his powerful arms holding up his muscled frame. In and out he moved, sliding through my copious wetness, the sound of our sexes moving past each other the most erotic symphony.

My arm remained around his neck, his blue eyes looking into mine in a way they never had before. They were clear like still water, like snowmelt flowing from the tallest mountain. His eyes could see through me, see my beating heart and the fragile ribs that kept it safe.

I pulled him close and kissed him, feeling that flush down my spine as well as between my legs. I never wanted this moment to end, this heated serenity, this instant where nothing else existed but the two of us.

I'd never felt so safe—emotionally or physically.

The explosion was immediate, my body tightening around him as I released all the stress, the pain, the past. My nails simultaneously dragged down as I gave a mixture of a whimper and a scream. "Benton…" His name was fire on my tongue. My eyes closed as I was pulled under the deepest water, a cool ocean that was as clear as air, except I could still breathe, breathe like I never had before.

My lips found his when it passed, desperate for another hit, for another out-of-this-world high that only he could give. It was just as potent as the drugs I had been forced to take, but the high was so much better, burned longer.

He met my hunger with his own, his lips taking the lead like he did with everything else. His fingers dug into my hair, and he thrust into me harder, my climax making his dick stiffen even more.

I could do this forever. Never stopping. Just going… on and on.

My ankles released and I tried to roll him onto his back, but he was too heavy, having the weight of an ox.

He rolled for me, taking me with him.

I straddled his hips, slipped his length back inside, and then sank deep.

He gave a suppressed moan as his jaw tightened, like it was the first time he'd entered me. His eyes closed briefly, his masculine face hard in desire. He propped himself up on his elbows and started to thrust from below.

My hands planted on his shoulders for balance, and I rolled my hips back and forth as I rode up and down, taking him from tip to base, over and over, feeling him stretch me every single time.

He didn't lie back and enjoy it. His body moved in sync with mine, his hips rising when I fell, a distinct smack of our bodies every time we came back together. His fingers gripped my knees as he watched me, taking in the sight of my shaking tits, of the sweat that coated my skin.

I made myself come again, and this time, he joined me.

I felt him release inside me—and it felt like a five-pound dumbbell. It made me wet all over again, to feel his arousal inside me, to have a piece of him. My body came to a halt, and I rested my forehead against his, his dick still hard inside me.

His lips caught mine, giving me an eager kiss like this was far from over. "Keep going."

I obeyed the command and rode his dick again, our arousal mixed together, smearing up his base as I moved up and down. My lips took his at the same time, my entire body on fire as if those climaxes had done nothing to douse the flames. It was as if we'd just started from the beginning—and that was a warm-up.

―――

HE DOZED off afterward on his back, his chest rising and falling at an even pace.

It took all my strength not to drape my arm over his stomach and rest my head on his shoulder. Every time I'd tried to have that kind of affection, I'd been met with the bite of rejection. He just wasn't that kind of man.

I propped myself up on my shoulder to look past him to the clock on his nightstand. I needed to leave to pick up Claire soon.

The movement must have stirred him because he opened his eyes and released a quiet sigh. His thoughts must have immediately gone to his daughter because his eyes darted to the clock too. He settled back down again, his fingers running through his hair as he stared at the ceiling.

"I'll get her. You can go back to sleep if you want."

"And miss ice cream?" His voice was deep and raspy, like he'd been asleep for the entire night instead of just thirty minutes. "Never."

I cracked a smile at his comment, liking the rare times when he made a joke.

He turned to look at me, his eyes still heavy like he was half asleep.

I could stare at those blue eyes forever. Throughout the night and the following day. Always. He was grizzled and bitter, but that somehow made me care for him more—because I was grizzled and bitter too.

We were the same person…in a complicated way. "Do you have to work tonight?"

"No. But I'll be out for a few hours."

"Oh." I wanted to ask where he was going, but I kept the question on my tongue since it was none of my business. If I asked, that was probably exactly what he would say. It would be the only time he'd left the house for a reason other than work, so it must be a social reason, but he didn't seem like a fan of socialization. I'd probably never know.

He got out of bed, standing there like a Greek god with that tight ass. He was muscled and chiseled, a gun without bullets. A black shirt was pulled over his head and then a long-sleeved flannel.

I watched him from bed, too comfortable to move, enjoying the view far too much.

Once he was fully clothed, he walked out without looking back.

And just like that, I felt it.

I felt the cold.

"I WANT A SUNDAE—"

"She'll take a single scoop." Benton looked down at her, his eyes narrowed in authority.

Claire turned to me and rolled her eyes.

I suppressed the chuckle as best I could.

"And that's not how you order," Benton said, pretending not to see what she just did. "Try again."

The young woman stood behind the counter and stared at Benton just the way I did, as if she couldn't believe a man like that existed.

Claire sighed. "May I please have a sundae—"

"One scoop of gelato in a cone."

Claire rolled her eyes—again.

This time, I brushed my hand over my lips because it was all I could do not to laugh.

The woman smiled. "You got it. What flavor?"

"Strawberry," Claire said.

Benton gave her a glare.

"Please," Claire said quickly.

We finished our order then took our ice cream to a table near the window. We all had the same thing, a single scoop on cones. Benton sat beside his daughter and spun the cone in his hand, dragging his tongue across the surface of the scoop. He would catch the cream on his tongue then swallow.

Damn.

His eyes caught mine when he felt my stare.

I quickly looked out the window.

"What kind did you get?" Claire asked with her soft little voice.

"Sweet cream."

Claire looked up at her father, strawberry ice cream all over her face. "Daddy?"

"Chocolate." He grabbed a napkin and wiped up her face. "And you're making a mess, sweetheart."

She shrugged and kept eating.

It was hard to believe this was my life now, in a beautiful apartment in Paris, living with a man and his daughter. Everything before the cult felt like a blur now. That life didn't seem real anymore. If I put on my ballet slippers, I probably wouldn't even know how to dance anymore. It was no longer my identity.

Whenever I looked out the window, I just enjoyed the view. I didn't search the streets for the skulls, for the cruel smile that haunted my dreams. As long as Benton was there, I was untouchable. He made me untouchable in other ways, too—from the cold, from the loneliness, the despair.

We walked back to the apartment as the sun started to set. It was a rare sunny day, and that made it even colder than usual. My breath escaped as vapor as I dug my hands into the pockets of my jacket.

Benton seemed immune to it.

When we made it back home, Claire got to work on her homework, and I sat with her and helped.

"Are you excited for Christmas?"

She nodded. "Christmas is my favorite holiday."

"Yeah, mine too." I looked at the tree near the fireplace, covered in lights and ornaments, a beacon of hope in these dark times. It filled the room with more warmth than the hearth.

"I wonder if my mom will come back for a visit." Her eyes were down on her worksheet, pushing the pencil into the paper as she did her basic arithmetic.

Helpless, I just watched her, a brand-new crack forming in my heart.

FOUR

Benton

THE DOORBELL RANG.

Claire was at the dining table working on her homework with Constance, and her concentration was immediately shattered when she heard the sound. "Who's that?"

I disappeared down the hallway and opened the door to see my brother on the other side. "Thought we were meeting there."

"And miss seeing my niece?" He stepped around me and entered the house without invitation.

The two of us returned to the main room, and my brother's eyes filled with warmth when he saw Claire sitting there. "Where's my favorite niece?" He was cold and callous like I was, but he turned soft for Claire. Something else we had in common.

Claire left her chair and ran into his arms. "I'm your only niece, Uncle Bleu!"

"Oh yeah, that's right." He hugged her into his chest and squeezed her tight. "You're so smart."

She hung on to his neck. "I know."

The chuckle that escaped my throat was instantaneous.

Bleu laughed too. "She really is your daughter, isn't she?"

"Damn right."

"Ooh." Claire pulled back and looked at me. "Daddy cussed…"

I gave a shrug in guilt before I looked at Constance.

She wore a look of relief that I couldn't explain. Like a boulder had been removed from her collar, her shoulders suddenly looked light. It was the same look she wore every time I came home, but I'd been at her side the entire day.

Bleu got to his feet and approached her. "Has she worn you out yet?"

Constance watched Claire come over to her with a look of fondness, and once she was close, Constance's arm moved around Claire's shoulders. "Nope."

"I'm her best friend," Claire said. "She loves me."

Constance chuckled and gave her a pat on the shoulder. "You're right about that, honey."

Bleu turned back to me. "Ready?"

"Yeah." I walked up to Constance. "Going out for a drink. I won't be gone long."

She nodded. "Have a good time."

I gave Claire a kiss on the forehead before I walked out with my brother. It was a frigid night without the blanket of clouds overhead, but every time that ice-cold breath hit my lungs, it felt like the smoke of a good cigar. Side by side, we walked, headed to our favorite dive bar—The Green Goose.

We took our seats at the bar, each ordered something strong, and then relaxed after the first sip.

"Are you sure she's your kid?" He swirled his glass as he surveyed everyone else in the bar. "Because she's the most adorable thing I've ever seen, and you're…you." He took a drink and caught the dribble at the corner of his lip.

"I don't know how I got so lucky either." She had my hair and eyes, but she didn't have my darkness and bitterness. Thankfully.

"Makes me want one…"

I turned my gaze on him.

"Someday."

I took a drink. "They're a lot of work."

"Yeah?"

"A lot of heartache."

"You seem happy."

"That's not how I mean it. When you love someone that much…it's hard. You're always worried. You're always living in the future but reflecting on the past. This little person relies on you for everything—and you can't fuck up."

"I wonder if it would have been easier if you weren't a single dad."

"A million times easier…as Constance has shown me." When I glanced at the other side of the bar, there were two women there, both staring in our direction. My eyes went back to my scotch, and I drenched my tongue.

"How are things with you guys?"

"Good."

Bleu stared at me. "I saw the way she looked at you."

I pivoted in the stool and met his look but gave nothing away.

"Guess she's not too traumatized after all."

I took another drink. "She came on to me, alright? Now drop it."

"Lucky son of a bitch…"

"You don't even know her."

"Know her? She's gorgeous. What else do I need to know?"

I sidestepped the comment by taking another drink.

My brother stared at the side of my face for a while, his glass on the counter. When he spoke again, his voice was serious, the taunts finished. "So, what is this? A relationship? Just a fling?"

"None of your business. That's what it is."

"Benton, come on."

I finished my glass then clanked it on the counter, needing another.

The bartender filled it again—and made it a double.

"How's the construction going?"

"It's not. Haven't taken a job in I don't know how long…"

"Are you going to shut it down?"

"I intended to juggle both, but I'm tired as fuck." Now I had two different personas. In the dark, I was a monster. But in the day, I was a doting father. "When Claire gets older and starts asking questions, I won't be able to keep up the pretense. But I won't be able to tell her the truth either."

"There's no way out of this?"

I shook my head.

"He's got enough men. What does he need you for?"

"It's complicated."

"You can't pay him off?"

"No. This was the price to save Claire—and I'll be paying it for the rest of my life."

Bleu looked down into his glass before he stared at the mirror behind the bar. The booze was stacked on glass shelves, the more expensive items closer to the top. With an elbow on the counter, his stare lingered. "Would it help if I took over the construction company?"

I turned to regard him.

"Would be easier to keep up the pretense that way."

"Got nothing better to do?"

"I thought I'd like retirement, but I'm a bit bored." His eyes stayed on the glass. "We got one on the hook. Wonder who she'll go for…"

It was one of the women sitting at the other end of the bar. Brunette with striking eyes and a tight dress, she strutted to our spot with the kind of confidence that implied this wasn't her first time making a pass at a stranger in a bar. "Hope it's you."

"I'm sure it will be."

She came right to my side, her arm resting on the counter. "I'm Francesca—"

"Leave me alone." My eyes remained on the mirror as I took a drink. Didn't look at her directly. Didn't acknowledge her.

My brother's eyes snapped wide open at my comment.

I didn't give a shit.

After a dirty look, she walked away.

When she was out of earshot, Bleu rounded on me. "What the fuck was that?"

"Didn't want to waste her time."

"But you didn't need to be a dick about it."

I looked into my glass before I took a drink. "I couldn't care less, man."

"Well, maybe she would have moved on to me if you hadn't scared her off."

"Then go talk to her."

Bleu remained in his chair, giving a slight shake of his head. "Things with Constance are pretty serious, then?"

I shrugged.

"Is that a yes or…?"

I gave another shrug.

"Fuck, just answer the question."

I pivoted on the stool and stared at him head on. "I don't know. As I already said."

"How do you *not* know?"

I gave a slight shake of my head. "It's complicated."

"Complicated, how?"

My elbow was propped on the bar, the closed knuckles against my temple. "It was supposed to be a one-time thing. But she didn't want it to be. I told her I had nothing to offer her, but she didn't care."

"So, it is a fling, then?"

I shrugged before I took a drink.

"Okay, stop doing that."

"No woman has ever loved my daughter more than she does. There's a connection between them…I can see it every time they're together. Sometimes I get angry. Angry that Beatrice was incapable of giving what Constance can so effortlessly." I stared into my glass. "But then I become grateful, grateful that our paths crossed the way they did…like it was fate."

My brother continued to watch me.

"Sometimes I wonder if she really is an angel. Claire's guardian angel. Because without her…" I stared into the dark liquid as horrible images flashed across my mind, tears streaming down my daughter's face while the monsters chased her from behind. "I met her once before, when I was looking for Claire. I didn't remember it, not until she told me about it. She's beautiful, but all beautiful women are unremarkable to me. But once I knew what she'd done for Claire…everything changed. She continues to do so much for my daughter, care for her in a way that I can't…because I wasn't there." I kept my eyes on my glass and felt my brother's piercing stare. "This shared experience has bonded us for life. The connection is the deepest one I've ever felt, second only to what I feel for Claire. I don't love her—but she's the only woman I could ever love."

My brother stared for a long time before he spoke. "Then it's definitely not a fling…"

―――――

WE LEFT the bar and walked back to my apartment.

"Are you going to kill him, then?" His hands were inside the pockets of his coat, his breath escaping as vapor. "I think you should—and I'd like to help."

"As much as I'd like to, my hands are tied."

"You really think he'll leave her alone?"

"He'd be stupid to cross me, especially after what Bartholomew said."

"Sure. Unless he moves against you first."

We approached the front door, and I stopped at the bottom of the stairs so we wouldn't be overheard. "One woman isn't worth it—even if he really believes she's an angel."

"Well, she's worth it to you, so…"

I stilled at the comment.

"Just don't drop your guard." He gave me a clap on the shoulder before he headed on his way. "Give Claire a kiss for me."

I entered the apartment and found the girls on the couch in front of the TV. Claire was snuggled with a pillow and blanket, dead asleep. The glow from the TV blanketed her face in blue light.

Constance lay on the other couch, still in her jeans and boots. Her makeup was smeared in places, as if she'd dozed off for a bit too. She slowly sat up and ran her fingers through her hair to pull it out of her face. Her light eyes met mine—beautiful and bright. They captured my focus and held it like the barrel of a gun.

I scooped Claire into my arms and carried her to bed. She stayed asleep as I carried her down the hallway and tucked her in for the night. I gave her two kisses on the forehead. One from me, and one from her Uncle Bleu. "Love you, sweetheart." I turned off the light and headed to the door.

Her incoherent mumbling followed me. "Lovyouto…"

That hot warmth moved down my throat and deposited into my heart. Like gaseous vapor, it expanded everywhere, getting into my lungs then circulating in my blood. She was the only person who could make me feel this way, joyous and heartbroken at the exact same time. I closed the door and returned to the living room.

Constance had cleaned up the area, folding the blanket and draping it over the back of the couch, fluffing the pillows, putting away the mugs of hot cocoa they'd enjoyed before passing out on the couch. When I returned to the room, I had her full attention. Her spine was straight and she was tense, but not tense in fear. It was almost like a soldier who stood at attention out of respect and admiration. "How was your night?"

She'd cleaned up her makeup while I'd been out of the room, so now the streaks of mascara were gone from underneath her eyes. But they still looked tired, like she was anxious for bed. I'd never appreciated her beauty before because I had more important things to worry about, but now I could see it. Whether it was her best day or her worst, her eyes glowed like the lights of the Eiffel Tower. Whether she was secure or scared, she was magnetic. "It was fine. What did you guys watch?"

"A Christmas movie. She was so hyper until we got the TV on. Then she was out like a light."

I gave a quiet chuckle. "You've discovered the secret weapon of parenting."

She chuckled too.

"Ready for bed?"

She ran her fingers through her hair again, getting it away from her face, doing something so simple but so elegant at the same time. She possessed a grace that seemed angelic at times. She always stood straight, always covered herself with subtle jewelry, always impregnated the room with her elegance the second she stepped into it. She gave a nod. "Can I sleep with you?"

I already had a girl who needed me for every aspect of her life. The last thing I wanted was to be emotionally responsible for another person, but with Constance, it didn't feel like a burden. The world was an unsafe place full of demons, and I was the one spot she could call home.

She needed me and wasn't afraid to show it. She used me to feel better—and I liked feeling used. I was a drug to her, a high she couldn't get anywhere else, a comfort no other man could provide. "I assumed you would."

Her exhale showed her relief, the way her lungs emptied as if she was about to drift off to sleep. There was always a look of appreciation on her face, like a night alone in her room was practically unbearable. I was the only thing standing in the way between her and Forneus—and the closer I was, the better.

We went into my room and got into bed. She stripped down to her thong before she got comfortable under the sheets, and I kept my boxers on as I slid into the spot beside her. Our passionate afternoon had been enough for me, and she seemed tired after falling asleep on the couch.

My sleep schedule was all over the place now, and after the afternoon nap I'd taken, I wasn't exactly tired. I turned on the TV and watched it on low, and she immediately knocked out on her side of the bed. She faced me on her side, the sheets pulled to her shoulder, and her breaths were instantly quiet, like it took less than a minute for her to fall into her dreams.

It took an hour for me to get tired enough to fall asleep, and I hit the button on the remote before I closed my eyes and felt my mind surrender to my dreams. But it seemed to last only a minute before I was pulled back into consciousness.

"It's not real…it's not real."

My eyes opened to see Constance beside me, her body shaking like she was cold, her eyes shut tight.

"No…I won't take it." Her arm flung out, fighting an invisible enemy, her lungs starting to gasp for air.

"Constance." I grabbed her wrist so she wouldn't accidentally smack herself in the face.

She threw her other arm too, trying to break free of my hold. "Fuck off!" She kicked in the bed, hitting me in the thigh under the sheets. "Die! Just fucking die."

I grabbed both of her wrists and pinned them against her stomach. "Come on, it's just a dream." I gave her a shake, pulling her out of her trance.

Her eyes flashed open, and she gave a deep gasp.

I kept the pressure on her wrists and held her in place.

She looked like a wild animal in the forest, running for her life, getting caught in the beam of a flashlight. She wanted to hop back into her hole and bury herself deep underground to safety.

"It's Benton."

Without blinking her eyes, she took me in, the vision slowly fading from her mind. With every breath, the rigid muscles of her body began to relax. Her resistance against my hands faded. A sense of safety washed over her when she recognized me, when she remembered where she was.

I let her go.

She darted for my chest, her arm circling my neck, her leg hooking over my hip. Her face found its place in the crook of my neck, her deep breaths dispersing across my skin.

My instinct was to push her off, but I chose to let her stay. I lay back on the pillow with her, her svelte body pressed against mine, her small tits near my chest. My fingers found their way into the back of her hair, and I stroked the strands as I waited for her breathing to go back to normal.

It did, but she didn't fall back asleep. I looked at the ceiling as I continued to stroke her hair, wide awake now that she was on top of me, making my personal space warmer than it usually was. "Just a dream."

"But my dreams…they feel like…"

"What?"

"Acid. When he forced me to take it, I never knew what was real or fake. I never knew if I was actually awake…or if I'd collapsed on the ground and dreamed the whole thing. There was a time when I ran in the forest, and demons were everywhere, Forneus in his real form, and I found this river… I thought it wasn't real. I plunged my hands into the stream, and it was ice-cold. I think it was real…but I'm not sure."

My fingers stopped playing with her strands as I pictured those men torturing the women they snatched off the streets. They became pets for their enjoyment. Dressed them up in ridiculous costumes and made them higher than a kite. Did they actually believe they were angels? Or did they just believe in their own power? It'd been a few months since she'd been away from the cult

—but she was no better than the day she'd returned. "You're safe now. They have no power over you."

"But I have no power over them either. All I have is you." She rested her cheek against my collarbone as her arm tightened around my torso. "I wish I could kill him. I wish I could kill them all. Then maybe I'd be able to get a good night's sleep…"

FIVE

Constance

I ARRIVED ON CAMPUS AND WAITED FOR THE BELL TO ring. It was a sunny day, and while the sunshine reddened my nose a bit, it was deceptive, because it was freezing cold. I was in my boots and jacket, my hands deep in my pockets.

When the bell rang, the children covered the grounds like ants emerging from a hill, and when Claire spotted me, she ran right toward me. This was our daily ritual now, and I loved it every single time. Her backpack bobbed up and down as she ran, and she made it into my arms. We embraced with a squeeze then broke apart.

"How was your last day?"

"It was good. We made paper Christmas trees and had pizza."

"Wow, that sounds like fun. I love pizza parties."

As we walked back to the apartment, she told me about her friends, that someone's mom was going to organize a gift exchange over the holiday break. When we got home, she set her backpack on the table and pulled out her artwork.

"I made this one for you."

"Oh, really?" I took it, seeing the paper ornaments and lights glued on the front. "It's beautiful, honey. I'll put it on the fridge." The appliance was already covered with pictures of Claire and other things she'd created throughout her life, so I found an open spot and secured a magnet over it.

"Where's Daddy?"

"He's still asleep—"

"I'm right here, sweetheart." His deep voice sliced through the air like a knife through the calmest water, and he emerged in his sweatpants and nothing else. His hair was matted in certain places because he'd just rolled out of bed. A six-foot-something hunk with gorgeous blue eyes, he was the sexiest man I'd ever seen.

It was hard not to stare.

He gave her a kiss on the forehead before he examined the other Christmas tree.

"That one's for you."

He took his time looking at it, admiring her craftsmanship as if it was a real piece of art. He was indifferent to the world around him, but whenever it came to Claire, he was completely smitten. A smile moved on to his face. "I love it." He did the same as I did and placed it on the fridge. "How about an after-school snack—"

"Mac and cheese!" She threw up her arms and followed him into the kitchen.

With affectionate eyes, he chuckled. "Alright."

I backed away from the room and entered the hallway because this was their time alone together. There were times when I belonged and times when I didn't, and I knew my place. I was supposed to take care of Claire when he was unable to, but if that was fulfilled, then I had no purpose.

"Constance?" Claire's sweet little voice came from behind me.

I turned back around.

"You want to help us make mac and cheese?"

"It's okay—"

Benton emerged behind her, a skyscraper that towered over her, and his blue eyes locked on to my face. He gave a subtle nod toward the kitchen then disappeared from view.

The smile that took up my face infected my heart at the same time. "Sure, I'd love to."

———

AFTER I PUT Claire to bed, Benton walked down the hallway in his jeans and a long-sleeved shirt.

I knew that meant he would be out of the house until morning—and it was always a disappointment. A jolt of anxiety hit me, along with a lot of other emotions too.

I walked him to the door. "Be careful."

His eyes regarded mine, shifting back and forth as he took me in. "Always."

"I wanted to say…I know it's kind of awkward, but…when you're with other women—"

His eyes grew angry, really angry. Just the look was enough to make my words die right in my throat. The look was livid, violent, full of rage. "I don't leave my daughter every night to fuck a whore."

"That's not what I meant—"

"Then say what you mean—and do a better job of it."

My arms crossed over my chest, and I felt myself cower because this was a version of him I hadn't encountered in a while. I'd gotten used to the version that I loved, the calm and open man who let me in… just a little bit.

"I know we aren't exclusive or anything—"

"I'm not sleeping around—if that's what you're asking."

My hands tightened on my arms, and I felt the relief fill my lungs when it shouldn't. "I wasn't asking, because it's none of my business—"

"I don't want to sleep with anyone else—so yes, it is your business."

My eyes locked on to his, the surprise making me go immediately still. There wasn't even a breath in my lungs. There wasn't a beat to my heart. I'd turned to stone.

After a long stare, he moved for the door.

My hand acted of its own accord—and reached for his arm. My brain didn't even have time to process what I was doing before it was already done. I pulled him toward me, pulled myself into him at the same time, and I found myself against his chest.

Instead of letting his arms hang by his sides as he rejected me, he encircled the small of my back and hugged me flush to his body, his chin resting on my head. He enveloped me with warmth, like his skin was my favorite blanket on the couch.

I rose on my tiptoes and planted a kiss to his lips, feeling that shock move all the way down my spine to every other inch of my body. My fingers dug into his arms, and I'd do anything to keep him there with me.

His hand cupped my cheek and brushed the hair from my face as he kissed me, taking the lead with his mouth, every kiss deep and purposeful.

My fingers tugged at his shirt, wanting it off his body and somewhere on the floor. I wanted that naked chest against mine, smothering me into the mattress while he moved deep inside me over and over. That high…there was nothing like it. "Do you have a couple minutes…?" I spoke against his lips, not wanting to break the trance that bound us together.

As if I was a box of feathers, he picked me up and carried me to his bedroom, kissing me the entire way. He laid me at the edge of his bed and pushed his jeans down so he could shove himself inside me.

Both of our shirts were on, and we clung to each other as he moved hard and fast, careful not to rock the headboard against the wall to wake up his daughter down the hallway. Our moans were suppressed to stay quiet, and our bodies became wet with sweat instantly. It was quick, desperate, animalistic.

It felt so good.

I said his name as I came, and the second he heard that word on my tongue, he released too, filling me as I climaxed. My hand tugged on his ass as I kept him inside me, feeling both his size and his load at the same time. "Benton…"

SIX

Benton

The silent auction was held at the museum, where priceless pieces of artwork earned bids worth millions of euros. Artwork was a currency for the rich, another way to display their wealth when the mansions and cars weren't enough. A piece was sold back to the community, and then another was purchased in its place. But it wasn't real estate, so it was worthless.

In my opinion.

Everyone was in gowns and tuxedos except the two of us. We were in our street clothes, but no one said a word to us.

Bartholomew and I stood in the corner together, and when a waiter walked up, he offered us each a glass of champagne.

I declined—because I didn't like that bubbly shit.

Bartholomew took a glass and a sip.

I watched him, already knowing how this was going to end.

He savored it in his mouth like it was a wine tasting—and then spat it back into the glass. He tossed it onto a nearby flower arrangement. "Yep. Piss."

"Then why did you take it?"

He shrugged. "Thirsty." He surveyed the room and gave a nod to one of the gentlemen. "Kline Weatherton. I'll be the good cop. You be the bad cop."

"You want me to shoot him?"

"Okay, not *that* bad."

"And our objective?"

Bartholomew ignored the question and crossed the room.

I tagged along, unsure if this would end in a civil conversation or gunfire. Either one was just as likely.

With a woman on his arm, Kline spoke to another pretentious man in a tuxedo.

Bartholomew made himself right at home and walked straight up to them both.

The conversation died instantly. Both men stared.

Bartholomew stared down the man on the right, the tension heavy for several feet in every direction.

Without saying a word, the man walked off, getting the message.

Kline released a sigh as he turned to the woman on his arm. "Why don't you make a bid on the paintings you like? I'll join you in a moment."

She was used to being told what to do—because she skirted off without question.

Kline took a drink of his champagne, probably just to wet his throat. "How can I help you?"

There had been several nights when my presence felt unnecessary. I could be home with my daughter, but Bartholomew liked having me around. I'd been out of the game a long time, but the people who remembered me from the good ol' days respected me, so it probably gave him an edge he didn't have when I was gone. "You remember Benton?"

I gave him a nod.

"Yes," Kline said. "It's been a while. What do you want?"

"No small talk, huh?" Bartholomew asked. "Good, because your yachts and mistresses don't interest me. I need you to set up one of your snob parties—me and Carlyle as your guests."

Kline glanced at the people around him from time to time, as if he was embarrassed to be seen talking to people in street clothes. Perhaps that was why Bartholomew bombarded him at that moment instead of having a phone call—it put the pressure on. "That bridge was made of steel, and you still managed to burn it down."

Bartholomew's stare was cold and hard, packed with a punch that didn't require a fist. "It needed a remodel."

"The answer is no, Bartholomew—"

"Then I'll host my own dinner party. Your wife and two mistresses. Should be fun."

Kline's face instantly blanched.

I gave a subtle shake of my head. "And I thought I was supposed to be the bad guy…"

Bartholomew ignored me, his dark eyes on his opponent. "Text me the details." His work finished, he walked away.

Kline watched him go before he turned to me. "Son of a bitch…"

SEVEN

Constance

Benton said I was welcome to his Range Rover to run errands, so I took the two of us shopping. I helped her pick out a couple gifts for her exchange with her friends, helped her pick out something for Benton, and I grabbed a few other things when she looked the other way. We pulled into the garage then walked into the house, my arms full of bags that we then sprawled out on the table.

"Can we wrap everything now?"

"Let's have lunch first. What do you want?"

"Hot dogs."

I chuckled and carried one of the bags toward my bedroom. "Try again."

"Why are you taking that bag away?" A curious child with a million questions, she fired away, inquisitive.

"It's just my makeup."

"I don't remember you buying makeup."

I should have done this shopping before she was home from school, but I hadn't planned ahead. Now that she was home every day, I had to find ways to keep her entertained, and while I liked having her around, it was also nice having her outside the house for a full day. A lot easier to get stuff done. "Never mind. Let's do the hot dogs."

Her eyes instantly lit up. "Alright." She moved into the kitchen to pull them out of the freezer.

I carried the bag into my bedroom and hid it in the closet so Claire wouldn't discover it by mistake. Once the door was shut, I turned to go, but I spotted something out of place on the nightstand.

It was a statue.

Of an angel.

Not a shiny ceramic one from a department store. This was made of real stone, with pieces of dirt still stuck to the bottom along with bits of moss.

My heart stopped, and then the jolt of sheer terror that followed immediately kicked it back into motion. My eyes darted to the window, which looked the same as I last saw it, and then the doorway, knowing we weren't alone.

I was instantly thrown back in time, back to the person I used to be, a survivor.

"Benton…" My hand reached for my back pocket and pulled out the phone, but the shakes were so bad that I dropped it on the floor before I could even get the light on.

That was when the front door opened.

There was no time to think. Only time to act.

I grabbed the knife in my nightstand then moved into the hallway. My knife raised with the intention to kill, I swung it before that grotesque smile could make me lose all my nerve. I would stab and stab until all his blood was drained and he was just bones.

My arm was thrown down, my wrist twisted, and then I was slammed into the wall. The air left my lungs when my back hit the solid surface. My eyes took in the man who'd bested me when he didn't even know I was coming.

Benton kept me pinned as he wore his look of rage. I couldn't move. I could barely breathe. Maniacal, he held me so tightly that he could squeeze the life out of me if he wanted to. He grabbed me so hard he bruised me in every place that he touched me.

The second I realized it was him, the air returned to my lungs. "He's in the house…"

His strong hands released my body, and he was gone. "Claire." He didn't raise his voice, but his command shook the house. He withdrew his gun from the back of his jeans and moved into the kitchen.

I seized the knife off the rug then held it at my side. The weapon brought me comfort, but I felt like I didn't need it anymore.

With her hand in his, he rounded the corner and brought her to me. "Stay here."

"Daddy…I'm scared." She hugged into my side, her arms snug around my hips.

He left us, his gun aimed, peering around the

corners and investigating every room in the house. Silently he went, his heavy footsteps not loud like they usually were when he made his way around the house.

The two of us remained huddled together, breathing heavily, anticipating the sound of a gunshot.

"What's happening?" she whispered. "Did…those scary men come back?"

I rubbed her back as I held her, my eyes still on the hallway. "It's okay, Claire. Your father will protect us."

It took a solid ten minutes for him to explore the entire house and the garage. When he was upstairs, I heard a subtle creak where the floorboards held his weight, but there was no other sound in the house. None of the windows were broken. The lock on the door wasn't busted. There was no trace of Forneus—but there never was.

Benton returned, his gun now stowed in the back of his jeans. "All clear."

Claire left my arms and ran straight for him.

I almost dropped my knife at his words. "Are you sure…?"

He picked her up and held her against his chest with a single arm. "Yes." He rubbed her back and pressed a kiss to her forehead, his eyes on me. He didn't ask any other questions, probably for Claire's benefit. "Sweetheart, everything is alright. No need to worry."

"Really?" she whispered.

"Yes. Didn't mean to scare you." He returned her to the floor and kneeled to give her an encouraging smile.

It was fake, but to a little girl, she didn't know the difference. "What'd you do today?"

Her arms stayed across her chest, and she swayed slightly. "Went shopping."

"Yeah?" he asked. "What did you get?"

"Christmas presents."

"You get anything for me?"

She started to lighten up at the questions, and this time, she gave a nod along with a smile.

"Tell me."

"But it's not Christmas…" She giggled.

"So?" He gave her a gentle tickle. "Come on, tell me."

She laughed and swatted his hands away. "No, Dad! You'll have to wait."

"Ah, man…alright." He got to his feet and gave her a quick rub on the head. "Hungry?"

She nodded.

"Go pick something out—"

"Hot dogs!"

He chuckled. "Alright, hot dogs, it is. How about you get everything ready?"

As if nothing had happened at all, Claire ran into the kitchen and started opening and shutting pantry doors.

The instant she was gone, Benton was back to business. His eyes were hard and demonic, and he stared me down as he demanded an explanation.

"I'll show you." I guided him into my bedroom and to the nightstand.

There it sat, cold stone, an angel without facial features. With my arms crossed over my chest, I stayed back, as if it were a bomb about to detonate.

Benton stepped forward, his gun poking out from the back of his jeans. He stared down at it for a while before he picked it up and examined it. He turned it over and stared at the bottom for a moment before he returned it.

"It was there when I came home…" The moment I dropped my guard, he came back. Just when I stopped searching for his smile, it returned. It came into my bedroom, in my space, in my home.

Benton turned back to me, his eyes smoldering with volcanic rage.

"I knew he'd never let me go…"

His eyes looked out the open doorway, where Claire continued to shuffle around looking for the buns. The TV eventually came on when she found the remote and turned on one of her favorite cartoons. "I have something to tell you." He wouldn't meet my gaze, which was unlike him.

All the muscles of my body clenched at the same time.

"About a month ago, I met with him."

My arms instinctively tightened across my stomach.

"He demanded that I return you."

"That motherfucker…" I shook my head, wishing I had stabbed my knife directly into his chest when I had the chance. I was free of that cult, but I was never free

The Catacombs

of him. It was an emotional imprisonment, psychological warfare.

"He made some threats, but my answer didn't change." His eyes came back to me.

"What kind of threats?"

He never answered. "I made my own in return—thought that solved the problem."

"Benton."

He held my stare.

"Answer me."

Stoic like a Roman statue, he held his silence.

"Oh god…Claire."

"I told him if he came anywhere near either of you, we would burn that cult to the ground."

I stepped back, my ragged breathing turning more labored. "I can't believe you didn't tell me—"

"Because I can handle it—"

"Obviously not!" My hands cupped my face and plunged my view into darkness because this reality was too much. My feet would feel that cold ground once again. Those wings wouldn't make me fly. They grounded me with their weight. The pill would hit my tongue, and I would ascend…into madness.

"Constance." His hands grabbed my wrists and pulled them down. "You need to calm down."

I pushed his hands away. "No."

He grabbed my wrists again, this time immobilizing me. "This is exactly why I didn't tell you."

I tried to fight his hold, but it was no use. It was like

a metal chain wrapped around both wrists. "Just give me back… I'm not worth it."

He looked down at me, his eyes injured.

"Don't feel bad about it. It's the right—"

"No."

"Claire—"

"You're both my girls, Constance."

I looked away, his words a bullet to the heart. "I took care of Claire because I wanted to. You don't owe me anything, Benton. I would do it again even if you'd shut that door in my face and never opened it again…"

His hands loosened on mine now that I was too heartbroken to fight. "And I would protect you…even if you hadn't saved my daughter."

Like the room was freezing, I crossed my arms over my body, hands latching on to my skin like cold, metal bars. That sentence was the single most profound thing he'd ever said to me, but my current turmoil made it impossible to appreciate.

He watched me for a while, a foot of separation between us. "He's just trying to get inside your head—"

"Well, he did."

"Don't let him—"

"You don't understand, okay?" My arms tightened over my chest, and I stepped away. "I had to entertain a madman, and when he offered me that pill or paper, I had no other choice but to take it. I don't know what's worse…being so high that I could drown in two feet of water or what happened afterward."

His eyes followed me as I paced.

I moved to the partially closed window, looking at the apartments across the street, wondering if he was in one of the windows staring at me right that very moment. "I should just go back—"

"No."

"He's not going to stop—"

"I will make him stop."

I turned back to him. "Then kill him."

His eyes faltered for just a moment, a brief look of hesitation. "You know I can't."

"Then kill Bartholomew."

"He's the reason both of you are here in the first place."

I gave a sigh as I dragged my hands down my face. "Then can I kill him?"

His eyes narrowed.

"There's no rule against that, right?"

He continued to stare.

"I'll go back with poison. Then I'll switch the papers when he's not looking—"

"No."

"Benton—"

"Daddy, are you coming?"

Benton gave an annoyed sigh, the first time he'd shown anything but affection for his daughter. "I'll be there in a few minutes, sweetheart." His eyes stayed on me, his mind still present in the conversation instead of dropping everything for her like always. "I will handle this."

"He was in the house—"

"When no one was home. That means he's watching us, so he's had every opportunity to take you and hasn't. Remember that."

"He was in *my* room." I threw my arms up. "I sleep in here—"

"Then sleep with me."

I felt his stern gaze on my face, felt it pierce every inch of my flesh. With every passing second, it became more difficult to remain upset, not when this man chased away my fear with just his words and intense stare.

"I'm not handing you over. And you aren't doing it voluntarily either. I will handle this."

My arms crossed over my chest again.

He stepped closer to me. "Alright?"

I had to tilt my head back to meet his gaze. When he was this close, he towered over me, towered over my heart. I gave a nod.

His powerful arms encircled my body and cradled me close, his chin moving to the top of my head, his warmth like a furnace. I was diminished by his size, belittled by his strength. It felt like a cocoon, but a cocoon of steel. "I want him dead too… You have no idea how much."

EIGHT

Benton

Bartholomew was never in the same place very long. He had apartments throughout the city and a large estate farther into the countryside. Unless his enemies had inside information about his whereabouts, it was like pulling a needle from a haystack. They'd be met with the Chasseurs, and even if they did make it out alive, it would all be in vain. Their cards would be on the table, and the consequences would be dire.

From the outside, there was no indication that one of the biggest kingpins in France was behind the sea of windows, drinking, fucking, sleeping, whatever the fuck he was doing. I let myself in, moved past the guards on the bottom floor, and made my way upstairs.

Women were everywhere.

French whores in lingerie were sprawled out in his living room. One lay upside down on the couch, a cigar in her mouth. She looked at me, pulled it out of her mouth, and then blew a cloud of smoke. Another sat with a drink in her hand, her legs crossed, her hair messy like Bartholomew had already had a go with her earlier in the evening. The girls standing at the counter immediately pivoted their bodies to face me, ready to proposition another client.

I didn't recognize any of them because it'd been seven years since I was last in the game. My bed used to be full of whores, too, in a different time, when it was just me and an obscene amount of money.

I didn't venture into the hallway because I knew what I would find if I continued—based on the sounds that carried to the living room. A woman moaning like she was there on her own time. Two, actually. And then a loud headboard to accompany it.

I helped myself to a glass of wine and leaned against the counter as I waited for him to finish up.

Like I was a carcass in the desert, the vultures descended. A blonde came first, the most confident one in the bunch, even though I barely gave her a second glance. She positioned herself right in front of me, one hand on her hip, in a black bustier with matching panties and thigh-high leggings.

"It's Benton, right?"

I took a drink of the Cab and switched my gaze to her.

"Bartholomew paid for us the whole night, so…"

"Leave me alone."

Her eyebrows rose up her face like she'd never heard that one before. "I think infidelity is good in a marriage. Keeps the man satisfied, which keeps the wife—"

"I said, leave me the fuck alone."

This time, her pretty face soured, and she strutted off like she was the one who had rejected me instead of the other way around.

The loud ruckus had stopped at some point, and Bartholomew emerged in just his black sweatpants, a gleam of sweat on his chest. He went straight for the wine like it was water after a hard workout. He tilted his head back, opened his throat fully, and took it all in a single swallow. Then he threw the glass against the wall. It gave a loud shatter, but none of the girls reacted, like they were used to this behavior. He wiped his mouth with the back of his forearm then sauntered over to me. "Help yourself—and not just to the wine."

I set down my glass. "We need to talk."

"You're awfully serious tonight." A few empty glasses sat on the counter, a small pool of red at the bottom of each, old glasses the girls had left when they'd switched to a new drink. He grabbed one and poured the bottle to fill it.

"After a freak breaks in to my apartment, it makes me pretty serious."

He took another deep drink like there wasn't already a pool of it in his belly. "What happened?"

"He left an angel statue on her nightstand."

"That's it?" He lifted himself onto the counter across from me, his hands gripping the edge as his glass sat beside him. The women seemed to know that this was business talk and kept their distance.

"*That's it?*"

"Trying to get all the information before I overreact—like you."

"If someone broke in to your apartment, you'd overreact too."

"No, if someone broke in to my place, I'd kill them. Why didn't you?"

"Because I wasn't home, asshole. No one was."

He grabbed his glass and took another drink. "So that freak came inside when no one was home to leave a toy? Pathetic."

"Well, my girl is scared."

"You told Claire?"

My glass suddenly felt heavy in my hand even though it was only half full. I grabbed the bottle and refilled it, just to have something to do with my hands.

Bartholomew could read everything on my face—he just didn't say it.

"He broke the truce. Now we kill him."

He gave a slight shake of his head. "Technically, he didn't break anything."

My eyes narrowed.

"You told him not to come anywhere near Claire and *your girl*." He looked at me over the rim of his glass as he took a drink. "There was no violation."

Now it was my turn to throw the glass down. It shattered all over the floor, and like last time, no one reacted. "Fuck off, Bartholomew. This motherfucker needs to die, and you know it. You made your threats, and you need to honor them."

"I know what I said, Benton. And clearly, he does too." He took another drink.

"I'm just supposed to deal with this freak stalking my family until he gets bored—"

"You could just give up the girl. Solves all your problems."

"Fuck you." The words spewed out of my mouth like vomit. All the muscles of my face suddenly felt strained because of the way my jaw tightened and pulled everything back. "I told you she's family—"

"No woman can fuck her way into being family. You're blindsided—again."

"What's that supposed to mean?"

"Claire came along and fucked up your entire life. Now you're letting this woman—"

"I will break this bottle and shove the neck into your throat if you say that shit again."

Bartholomew kept up his stare, his shoulders relaxed like he wasn't afraid of the glass spikes that would penetrate his tissue and bone. "We say how it is. It's always been that way—and I'm just being real with you."

"And I'm being real with you—don't talk about my daughter like that."

"Fine." He raised his arms. "But this woman is not off-limits. If you were smart, you would just throw her back to the wolves."

"She. Saved. My. Daughter."

"Whatever."

"You're all about loyalty—and you expect me not to be loyal to her?"

"You weren't loyal to me."

I clenched my jaw tighter because I would always be on the hook for this. "I had to do the right thing for my daughter. Don't expect me to apologize for that. I won't."

"You're here right now, aren't you?"

"Because I have to be—not because I want to."

He gave a cold chuckle. "Ouch…"

"And because I have someone at home with her while I'm away. Beatrice was a piece-of-shit mother."

"She's a piece of shit to you, but to me, she was someone pressured into something she didn't want. Very different things."

There were a million things I could say, but they were things I'd already said. Our relationship had improved, but the resentments he carried still drove us apart. He'd never forgiven me for what I did, not really. "Let me kill him."

"No."

"So, you didn't mean a damn thing you said?"

He took another drink of his wine. "I mean every word that I say. So, if he crosses the line, we make our move. But he hasn't done that. Like I've said a million times, he may be a freak, but he's a smart freak."

"So, that's it?" I asked with a hard jaw. "I just deal with this shit?"

He gave a shrug. "He'll get bored eventually."

"And I'm just supposed to wait?"

"I mean…you know what your other option is."

My eyes shifted away because that wasn't an option at all. "I want to talk to him—set up a meeting."

Bartholomew stared at me, the muscles of his hard body tightening. "Don't be stupid, Benton."

"I'm not going to kill him."

"What will that accomplish—"

"*Just set up the fucking meeting!*" I slammed the bottle onto the floor, the glass shattering and spilling the contents of red wine.

Bartholomew didn't even flinch.

I walked off, finished with all this bullshit.

His voice trailed behind me. "Ladies, I think my friend here needs a pick-me-up. Any volunteers?"

I didn't turn back. "Fuck off."

WHEN I WALKED in the door early in the morning, Claire was still asleep.

Constance lay on the couch, her head propped on a pillow she'd taken from her bed, a blanket pulled to her shoulder. The lights were still off, and the Christmas tree glowed in the corner.

She didn't hear me walk in, probably because she was exhausted from being awake all night, so I stirred her with the sound of my voice. "Constance."

Her eyes opened, and she instinctively reached for the knife on the coffee table, the souvenir she'd brought back from the cult. With a heavy breath, she jolted upright, locked her gaze on me, and then closed her eyes in relief.

I fucking hated this.

She loosened her grip on the knife and returned it to the table. "Sorry…"

I shifted her blanket over and took the seat beside her.

She took a couple minutes to wake up, to let the terror circulate out of her blood.

"He won't come into the house while you're here."

"How do you know that?"

"Because those were the terms—not to go anywhere near either of you."

Her eyes were red and tired, like she didn't sleep at all last night.

"Don't be scared."

"I wish he would come into the house…so I could kill him."

Even with a weapon, she didn't have much of a chance. He was a big guy—and he was smart. "You won't need to after I talk to him."

She slowly turned to me, her eyes wide. "When?"

"I don't know yet."

"I want to come."

"We can't kill him, Constance."

"Maybe I can plead with him…"

"I think if he speaks to you, it'll just make it worse. I'll take care of it."

She dragged her hands down her face before she

rubbed the sleep from her eyes. "I guess I should make breakfast."

"I'll take care of it. Get some sleep."

"You've been out all night—"

"And you've been up all night. I can take care of Claire."

"You're sure?" She turned to me, beautiful vacancy in her gaze, like she really was too tired to be fully present in the conversation. There were bags under her eyes, a tightness to her skin. But there was something about the way she looked early in the morning. This was one of the first times I'd gotten to see it.

I gave a nod.

"Can I take your bed…?"

I nodded again. "Always."

"DAD, we don't have any cookies." Claire looked through the pantry, pushing aside cans of soup and boxes of cereal.

"Because we don't need any." She'd always had a sweet tooth, but I could barely tolerate the stuff. I joined in on the festivities like getting gelato after school just to bond with her, but it'd never been my thing. If a wine was too sweet, I didn't like that either.

"What about Santa?"

"We'll get some before he comes." I stayed on the couch, one of her favorite shows on, our coloring books on the coffee table. I prided myself on being a good father, but I did drink when she was around, whether that was wine or scotch. It never inhibited my faculties, so it wasn't like I was an absent parent.

"Dad, he's coming tonight." She ran back into the living room, giggling because she knew something I didn't.

"Tonight?" I asked. "Wait…"

"It's Christmas Eve!"

Shit. "It is?" I pulled out my phone and checked the calendar.

"Santa is coming tonight, and we don't have any cookies. What if he doesn't leave any presents?"

"He will. I'm pretty sure he's full of cookies by the time he gets here."

"But if I don't have cookies, he'll think I'm a bad girl."

"No, sweetheart." I brought her in for a hug and kiss on the forehead. "He could never think that. But we'll make some anyway—just to be safe."

"Yes!"

"What should we make?"

"Those cookies that we decorate."

"Sugar cookies?"

"Yep."

"Alright." I got off the couch and headed to the kitchen. "Let's see what we've got."

"Constance, we're making cookies!"

She came into the living room, still in her tight leggings and a baggy shirt. Her eyes were still sleepy, but not exhausted like they were before. "You are? That sounds like fun."

"Daddy forgot that Santa is coming tonight."

"He did?" she asked with a chuckle. "That sounds about right…"

"Come on, help us." Claire grabbed her hand and pulled her into the kitchen.

We worked together to make the dough, cut them into Christmas trees, reindeer, and gingerbread people, and then put them in the oven. After they cooled, we used the colored frosting to decorate.

"Look at my tree." Claire showed Constance her creation.

"Very nice," she said. "What do you think of my reindeer?"

Claire stood on her platform so she could reach the counter, and she leaned over to see the cookie on the sheet. "What's that red thing?"

"His nose," Constance said.

"Ooh," Claire said. "That's really cool."

"What about mine?" I'd made a sled by mixing red and black together for a really deep color.

Claire gave it a disapproving look. "I don't like it."

I grinned and put it down. "Just not as good as you are, sweetheart."

Once all the cookies were decorated, the afternoon was long gone, and now it was dark outside.

"I'll clean up everything and start dinner," Constance said. "You can sleep for a couple hours."

"I'm alright." I dusted off my hands before I crumpled the parchment sheets and tossed them.

"Does that mean you'll be home tonight?"

"I was supposed to go out, but I didn't realize it's Christmas Eve."

Her eyes lit up, like that was the best news she'd heard in a while. "Great."

ONCE CLAIRE WAS PUT to bed, I took a couple bites out of the cookies and left the plate on the coffee table.

Constance walked out, carrying a handful of wrapped Christmas presents.

I'd totally dropped the ball on Christmas this year. Had too much shit going on. Stretched too thin. But she'd picked up the slack.

She put the presents under the tree, most of them addressed to Claire. There was one for me too.

Guilt dropped into my stomach. "I didn't get you anything."

There was no hurt in her eyes, just a smile. "Yes, you did. You gave me Christmas." She sat beside me. "You gave me a home. It doesn't come in a box with shiny ribbon, and it certainly doesn't fit under the tree…but it's the greatest gift anyone has ever given me." She stared at the tree for a while, taking in the twinkling lights and the presents she'd just stuffed underneath. Then she slowly turned to me, and that same look of wonderment remained on her face.

As with every time I looked at her face, I found something new to appreciate. Right now, it was her affection, the way she made me feel warm without even touching me, the way she made this home better than when it was just Claire and me.

"Ready for bed?"

Her eyes remained glued to mine as she gave a subtle nod.

The lights were flicked off, and the bedroom door was shut behind us. Before I even had a chance to get my shirt over my head, she was on me, yanking on the button of my jeans to get them off. Her lips pressed against my chest, and she kissed me, dragging her tongue over my hot skin, her fingertips pressing into my muscles.

I got her undressed, pushing her leggings over her perky ass and dragging her thong along for the ride. Clothes littered the floor until it was just our bare feet against the rug. Our mouths came together in a hot embrace, packed with tongues and heat, her nails clawing at my back.

I got her onto the mattress, my hips fitting between her soft thighs that opened to me like a flower on the first day of spring. The bed dipped from our weight, and the sheets hugged her slender body underneath me. I guided myself inside her, giving a moan when I felt how wet she was, when I felt how much she wanted me.

She always wanted me.

She scooped me closer to her and hugged my hips with her thighs, keeping me in place so she could enjoy my thick entrance. A breathy moan escaped her mouth, her nails digging deep as if that was all she needed to feel good—me.

My thrusts started off slow, enjoying the way her arousal smeared me from base to tip, the way she was wet just from being in the same room with me, just from looking at me, just from hearing my voice.

The sex was so good, it was like I paid for it.

She cradled me close and kissed me as she rocked back into me, her anxious lips desperate for my mouth with every embrace. Her little tongue glided past mine, and she moaned directly into my mouth, doing her best to stay quiet when she was getting the best sex of her life.

I assumed it was—based on the way she drew blood with her nails.

I could feel her climax before it came, feel the subtle ripples in her body as it began to crumble. The deep vibrations continued until her body squeezed mine with an iron fist.

"Benton…" She smothered her lips against my neck, suppressing her moan as much as possible, keeping our passion confined to the bedroom. Her hand tugged on my ass next as she rode the high as long as possible, keeping me deep inside her as she finished.

I wanted to keep going, to make her come like that all over again, need me more than she already did, but the heat was too much. It had started the moment I'd felt her wet tightness, and I'd been holding back this entire time. There was nothing like walking through the front door and coming inside the woman who couldn't sleep without you, who listened for the door until you were at her side once again, who wanted your climax as much as you wanted to give it.

Deep between her legs, I released with a loud moan that shouldn't have left my lips. I enjoyed every second, the way it tingled all the nerves of my spine, the way it made my balls tighten, the way it made me forget everything but the two of us. She dug her fingers into the back of my head as she watched me finish, her eyes still hot. She hugged me against her and kissed me, a hot, wet kiss full of passion that hadn't extinguished.

I was used to women wanting me, but I'd never been wanted the way she wanted me.

I rolled over and lay there, my eyes heavy with a new wave of exhaustion. The space didn't last for long because she snuggled into my side, her arm around my waist, her head on my shoulder.

This time, I didn't push her away.

I'd never push her away again.

———

"DADDY, HE CAME!" Claire tried to turn the knob, but it was locked. "Santa came."

My eyes opened to see Constance in the same place I'd left her, on my chest and in my arms. I took a breath before I turned to look at the clock.

7:45.

Jesus Christ. "Be there in a second, sweetheart."

"Hurry!" Her feet pounded against the hardwood floor as she bolted for the living room.

When Constance was awake, she sat up in bed and ran her fingers through her long hair. She looked at the clock too and gave the same reaction I did. "She slept in yesterday."

"No kid sleeps in on Christmas morning."

We both got dressed in our pajamas and came into the living room, where Claire was crawling around the bottom of the tree looking at all the presents Constance had placed after she went to bed. "See, Dad? What if we didn't put those cookies out?" She walked over to the plate. "Look at how many he ate."

I gave a nod. "You were right, sweetheart."

"He might eat a lot of cookies, but I bet mine are his favorite."

She made my heart grow bigger every day, and it grew a little bigger even now. I kneeled and gave her a hug and kiss. "They are."

She was quick to squirm out of my embrace because she cared far more about the gifts than my affection. "Can we open them?"

"Yes."

She grabbed them and divvied them up, making a pile for each of us. "I have way more presents than you guys…" Her eyes dropped in guilt because that was the kind of kid she was. She wanted everyone to have enough—not to have more than everyone else.

"Because we aren't kids anymore, sweetheart. So, enjoy it while you can." I made us coffee before I sat beside Constance on the couch and watched my daughter open her gifts on Christmas morning. I used to do this alone every year. Just the two of us. But this new tradition was nice.

She got lots of clothes, new toys, a full set of markers for her coloring books, and a book of pony stickers. Constance had gotten everything on my list, and it brought me so much joy when Claire loved my things more than everything else.

She grabbed another gift and read the tag. "From Mom… She sent me something." She pulled it close and started to rip through the paper with excitement.

My eyes immediately went to Constance.

She kept her eyes on Claire and ignored mine.

Claire got to the box and pulled out a collection of glass horses, more like works of art than toys, something to put on her shelf to admire whenever she worked at her desk. "Wow…these are pretty." She grabbed each one and examined it, taking care of them like she understood how fragile they really were.

"Looks like there's a note right there." Constance pointed to the tag, which had fallen off as my daughter had ripped everything to shreds.

She picked it up, squinted, and read. "Merry Christmas, Claire. Love you so much. Mom." She dropped the note and immediately went back to her new prized possessions, a happy kid on Christmas morning.

I looked at Constance and conveyed everything that I wanted to say with a look.

She finally met my eyes, sadness in her gaze, like her

ploy wasn't enough to drive away the sorrow. She felt for my daughter the way I did, like we really were two players on the same team.

My hand went to her thigh, and I leaned in close. My fingers squeezed her pajama-clad leg as I let my face hang there close to hers, seeing the way her breathing picked up with my proximity. Then I leaned in and kissed her—not caring if Claire saw.

NINE

Constance

We spent the day watching Christmas movies while Claire played with her toys on the floor. Clothes seemed to be the least important thing to her because she didn't touch them, not even the new pajama set I'd bought her. Everything Benton had asked me to get seemed to be her favorites, and it made me happy to know that he knew her better than anyone.

Benton had pulled me close on the couch, his arm around my shoulders as he let me cuddle with him under the blanket. Sometimes I dozed off, sleeping on this rock-hard man like he was the softest pillow in the world.

When the doorbell rang, I gave a jerk.

"Who's that, Daddy?" Claire asked.

"Uncle Bleu." He left me behind on the couch and went to the front door.

The guys returned a moment later, his brother

carrying a couple presents. "Where's my favorite niece?"

"Right here!" Claire ran right up, but instead of giving him a hug, she just took the presents and sat on the floor.

Bleu took it in stride and gave a laugh. "Merry Christmas, Claire." He took a seat on the armchair while she ripped everything apart, giving yells of delight when she found things she liked. He was in a dark coat with dark jeans, looking like his brother in several ways, but distinctly different with his own features.

Benton handed him a mug of hot cocoa.

Bleu took a look at the marshmallows floating on top before he gave a grimace in disappointment.

Benton chuckled and gave him a pat on the shoulder. "Just try it."

He brought it to his lips and took a drink. At first, there was a cringe, but then he took another sip. "Hmm…not bad."

Benton returned to the couch beside me, his hand absentmindedly going to my thigh as he watched his daughter open presents from her uncle.

Bleu noticed too and gave a smirk.

Claire made a brand-new mess on the floor, full of boxes and wrapping paper, her gifts the only things that survived the massacre. She squeezed the soft teddy bear to her chest. "Thank you, Uncle Bleu."

"You're welcome, sweetheart." With his mug in his hands, he watched Claire play with her things, just the way her father had watched over her earlier that morning. "Miss school?"

She gave a dramatic shake of her head.

He chuckled. "I didn't care for school either."

"I just love Christmas," Claire said. "I don't want it to end…"

"Well, there's always next year."

She lifted her head, as if a thought popped into her mind. "We made cookies. You want one?"

"Um, I'm not a big fan of sweets." He rubbed his stomach as he gave a shake of his head.

"Come on, Uncle Bleu." She ran into the kitchen to get more from the cookie jar. "We made them ourselves." She returned with a handful, some of Benton's dark cookies and the rest the bright, cheerful ones she and I'd made together.

He cracked under peer pressure and ate one. "Wow, you're right…they're good."

She waved her finger at him. "Told you." She dropped back onto the floor to her toys again.

I looked at Benton's brother. "Would you like to stay for dinner?"

"No thanks." He shook his head. "Got plans."

"What kind of plans?" Benton asked.

He gave a shrug. "A date."

"On Christmas?" Benton asked.

Bleu gave him a staredown that told him not to ask questions.

Benton gave a slow nod, like he got the message. "Have fun with that."

"Oh, I will." Bleu smirked then took a drink of his cocoa. "No work for you?"

"There's always work, but I'm not going." Benton watched his daughter, his only focus.

"Bartholomew was cool with that?" he asked.

"I don't care what he's cool with," Benton said. "I do what I want—when I want."

———

CLAIRE KNOCKED OUT PRETTY EARLY, probably because of all the excitement of the day. She put on the new pajamas I'd given her, so I guess she did like them after all. Once she was tucked in for the night and the house was cleaned up, we went to bed.

I could feel his mood like an oven. It turned on and slowly filled the room with heat, getting warmer and warmer. He was a man of few words but very palpable energy. He sat on the edge of the bed in just his sweatpants, his bare feet on the rug, his powerful physique hard and straight. His arms rested on his knees, and his hands came together between his thighs.

My fingers slid across one shoulder, the enormous hunk of muscle, and then to the back of his neck. My fingers lightly grazed through his short hair, and that jolt of electricity was instant, shocking me down to my toes.

He kept his head down, lost in thought, his mood bitter.

I broke his hands apart and lowered myself to my knees between his, meeting his stare now that I was where his eyes had been a moment before. My hands gripped his thighs and slowly moved up, gliding over the fabric of his sweatpants, toward the hard lines of his stomach.

His eyes remained on mine and didn't react to my touch.

"Are you mad at me about the gift?"

He didn't give any kind of reaction, but his answer was still apparent.

"I should have asked you first, but…I didn't want to bring it up."

"You did the right thing. I should have thought of it myself."

"You've got a lot going on right now."

"Doesn't matter. I'm a father first."

"Well, don't forget you have me too. You don't have to be responsible for everything."

His eyes stared into mine, deep and blue, beautiful like the rest of him. The look used to be unnerving, but now, it was my happy place, a place I could get lost in for hours. "You're the best thing that's happened to us—both of us. I'm just sorry for the way it came about." He dropped his gaze, probably thinking about the same thing I was thinking.

"It was worth it."

His eyes flicked back up to mine.

"I would do it all over again…"

The stare continued, deep and hard, like he saw me

in a whole new light. "I'll kill him. I don't know when… but I will. I promise you."

"What about the camp?"

"I'll burn it to the ground—turn it to ash."

I nodded.

"His death is for Claire. But everything else…that's for you."

———

THE HOLIDAY BREAK PASSED QUICKLY. Claire and I spent a lot of time together, and she spent a lot of time with her father too. We made a trip to the stables to visit their horses in the rain, took down the Christmas tree after the new year, and then the house was back to its usual state. Now, it was just winter…gray skies and slick sidewalks.

I'd been living in this winter a long time.

When I'd arrived at the cult, it'd been the beginning of fall. Months passed, and that cold deepened, the ground feeling like ice against my bare feet. But even if spring had arrived, my mind would have been forever trapped in the cold.

I hadn't returned to my bedroom since the incident. Whatever Benton did with the statue…I had no idea. All I knew for sure was that it was out of the house. That night when I looked out the window and saw Forneus's face…I'd wondered if that was real.

It was still hard to know what was real and what wasn't.

I had just finished the dishes in the sink when the front door opened. My ears immediately strained for the sound of his heavy footsteps, his gait slow like he was never in a hurry.

I finished with the dishes as I heard him behind me, felt his heat around me, felt a presence so palpable it felt as if it was inside me. As if I had eyes in the back of my head, I knew he was behind me, knew exactly where he was.

Then his hands gripped the counter on either side of me, and his chest pressed into my back. Pine needles. Bar soap. The smell of man. It felt like the stove was on because the kitchen suddenly became much warmer.

My head turned over my shoulder to regard the man who towered over me, seeing those bright-blue eyes piercing into mine. Possessive. Intense. Deeper than the deepest part of the sea.

My hands dried on the towel as I held his stare. "How was your night?"

His eyes remained steady as he cupped the side of my face and pulled me closer. He leaned in and kissed me, a slow kiss packed with purpose. His neck angled farther to meet my shorter stature. When the kiss was over, he left me there and headed to the fridge to help himself to the leftovers.

I was paralyzed—because he'd never done that before.

He never kissed me when he walked in the door.

He ate his food cold and paired it with a glass of scotch. His heavy body occupied one of the chairs at the dining table, and whether he liked his meal or not, it wasn't clear. He devoured everything that I served him, even the stuff that Claire didn't like.

I sat across from him and watched him, watched the way he hunched over his food, the way his large size made the table creak underneath the weight of his arms. Whenever he had a big bite in his mouth and he chewed, he would study my gaze, study me exactly the way I studied him.

"When are you going to talk to him?"

He finished his bite and washed down the eggs with a drink of his scotch. "Tonight."

My chest automatically seized, like every muscle tightened all at once.

"And how do you think that'll go?"

He took another drink of his scotch. "I'll take care of this, alright?"

"What if he—"

"I said, I'll take care of it."

"I just… I don't want you and Claire to go through this—"

"Claire doesn't know a thing."

I released a painful sigh.

His plate was clean, so he set his fork on top and held my gaze. "It may not happen tonight or tomorrow. But I will make this go away. And even if I can't, he'll move on to someone else eventually."

Images flashed across my mind, the cold statues in the center of the camp, Beatrice's blood on the dais as she was carved like a roast, the women in their gowns in the church, playing pretend to stay alive. "That'll make me feel better…but not by much."

His eyes narrowed, as if he didn't understand.

"Someone will take my place…and suffer the way I suffered. The cycle will continue, the graveyard will run out of vacancies, and then they'll make a new graveyard…for all the women who come after."

With his elbows on the table, he stared at me.

"It'll never really end…"

His eyes were steady, and instead of his usual flash of irritation, there was something else. "It will—someday."

I dropped my chin and looked at the table between us.

"Baby."

The air that was yanked into my body was involuntary. My lungs expanded on their own, gulping the oxygen my blood suddenly craved. My eyes remained down, the echo of his voice reverberating in my head. It wrapped around me like a piece of armor, a bulletproof vest, the kind of affection I'd never known.

He held his silence, waiting for me to raise my chin again.

I finally did, and it was hard to look him in the eye when he looked like that. Intense. Commanding. Powerful.

"You have my word."

TEN

Benton

I got Claire ready for bed and tucked her in for the night.

She pulled her new stuffed bear against her chest and turned on her side to face me.

"What's his name?"

"Bleu."

I smirked. "Looks just like him too."

She gave a chuckle as she squeezed him tighter.

I tucked the blanket around her to keep her warm then ran my hand over the top of her hair, catching some of the soft strands.

Her eyes always turned tired when I did that. They started to blink now. She tried to keep them open, but the fatigue was too much. It was a pointless battle, but it happened every night, nonetheless. When she was a baby, she would fight it even more, and we ended up with a lot of crying fits.

When her eyes closed, they stayed closed this time.

I gave her a kiss on the forehead.

"Daddy...?" Her eyes remained closed, her bear against her chest.

"Yes, sweetheart?"

"Can Constance be my mommy too?"

I stared at her innocent face as I stilled on the spot.

Her eyes opened when she didn't get an answer.

"If you want her to be."

She closed her eyes again.

I watched her for a moment longer before I let myself out of her bedroom. Constance was on the couch in the living room, ready to say goodbye before I left for the night. In her leggings and a loose-fitting shirt, she was comfortable for the evening but still stunning to me. She rose to her feet when I came close, ready to walk me to the door.

I held her stare for a moment.

"What is it?"

After a quick deliberation, I gave a shake of my head. "Claire just told me she loves you... That's all."

Her eyes softened like a wilted flower, and the depth of that love went well below the surface, into the recesses of her heart. "I love her too."

I'd never had a woman anywhere near Claire, but I imagined if I had, they would've tried to use my daughter to earn my affection. It would be a superficial ploy just to get to me. But I never had to worry about that with Constance—because she loved my daughter before she even knew me.

"Don't go..." Her eyes pleaded with me to stay. She

wanted every night to be the same—with the two of us in that bed. Sex. Sleep. More sex in the morning. And then the rest of our day.

I wished I could give it to her. "This is the only kind of life I can offer you."

She gave a nod, but her eyes were depressed.

"This isn't the life I want for us either. I don't want my daughter to grow up with an absent father."

"You aren't absent, Benton."

"But I'm not present either."

"Do you think…this is forever?"

Probably. "He told me the price for Claire—and I paid it."

"But you guys are friends, right?"

"More than friends, but not anymore."

"Then he should have helped you with no compensation." She came forward, her arms crossed over her chest. "A man is missing his daughter, and you take that as an opportunity to exploit him?"

"It's a lot more complicated than that."

"How?"

"I founded the Chasseurs with him a long time ago. It was ours. No wives. No children. That was our vow—and I broke it."

"Sounds like he just needs to shut up and get over it."

"And he would have…but I left to take care of Claire."

"I know, but I don't see why that's such a betrayal."

"I turned my back on him. That's why."

She gave a shake of her head. "He's a big boy. He can handle business without you."

"Like I said, it's more complicated than that. He was more like my brother than Bleu's ever been. It's probably hard to believe, but…we used to be totally different. The men who work for you are only there to earn some money. You can't buy loyalty. And you can't earn it by being their boss either. I was the one person he could trust implicitly—and I walked away. I'm sure it's been a lonely existence ever since."

She kept her arms crossed over her chest, not an ounce of pity in her eyes. "Maybe you can change his mind at some point."

"Only if I could offer him something no one else could."

"Then find something to give him."

WE WERE BACK at the Louvre, the January fog blurring the lights in the haze.

Bartholomew sat beside me in the back seat at the curb, the steps between the lampposts slick with earlier rain. He looked out his window for a while before he regarded me. "You shoot him, I shoot you. Got it?"

I held his gaze. "You're full of shit."

"Then let's find out." He got out of the car, pulled his pistol from the back of his jeans, and cocked it with a menacing stare.

Our previous friendship may have been in tethers, but I didn't buy that for a second.

I joined him, and we headed up the stairs.

He was exactly where I saw him last, surrounded by his freakish cronies with the skulls, dressed in all black. The second I came into view, his eyes shifted around me, as if I would cave that quickly. When he realized she wasn't there, the anger set in, made his face heavy, made his eyes coarse.

The fog was so thick, the Louvre was difficult to see. The fog was a sea, so heavy it made the surrounding buildings look like erased pencil on a page. With every breath, we inhaled the cloud, the moisture lining our lungs.

He seemed bigger than last time, the cords in his neck popping because his flesh was so tight around his musculature. He stepped forward, all his focus on me. There was a slight tremor to his body, the kind that made his head shake left and right slightly, like he couldn't contain this level of rage.

"The agreement has changed. Come on to my property again—and war is declared."

Bartholomew turned to me, wearing an identical look of rage to Forneus.

I knew if he objected verbally, he would look like he'd lost control of his own men, so it was better to keep his mouth shut and deal with me later.

Forneus started to shake harder, the energy filling his body to full capacity then pouring out when it had nowhere else to go. "*She was mine first!*" The shout echoed everywhere in the plaza, like a gunshot that split the night and woke up an entire neighborhood. His hands were in tight fists, and his head was dropped forward slightly, like a ram about to charge. He inched closer, like this had just turned into a fighting ring. "Give her ba-ck to-me." When his tone dropped, it was more sinister than the shout because of how eerie it sounded. "I can't ascend without my an-gel—"

"Get another one and move on."

"Get *another*?" His head cocked slightly, and he came a little closer. Now we were just a few feet apart. "If that's s-so ea-sy, why don't you?"

"You risk your entire enterprise for a woman who can easily be replaced. Find another angel. Forget about her—"

"I will never forget her!" He came closer still.

I didn't need the knife in my pocket or the gun stuffed in the back of my jeans. I could kill him with my bare hands. "Come on to my property again, and I will take away what you have left. You've been warned."

He started to shake again, his face stretched back as the grimace set into all his features.

I turned my back on him—the discussion over.

"Ben-ton."

I stilled at the way he said my name, like I was truly trapped in a horror story.

"Who will pro-tect Cla-ire when you're dead?"

I slowly turned back around to face him.

"Now *you've* been warned."

BARTHOLOMEW WAS STONE SILENT.

Didn't say a word on the drive.

Didn't say a word when we entered his apartment.

Didn't say a word as he poured himself a drink.

He was a time bomb set to go off—but he was the only one who knew exactly when. He brought the short glass to his lips and took a drink as he stared at me over the rim.

"He's afraid of us, Bartholomew. Use that to your advantage."

"*My* advantage?" He set the glass down. "I need no advantage because I have no qualms with these freaks. They're business associates—good ones. And you're pissing all over that when you can pay for pussy twice as good as hers."

"Don't talk about her like that."

"Claire's off-limits, and now so is she—"

"Yes."

He gave a dramatic roll of his eyes. "Pathetic. Where's the Benton I used to know? Where's the man who could carve the eyes out of a guy who cut us off in line? Where's the man—"

"He's dead—and he's not coming back."

He grabbed the bottle and poured more into his glass.

"Your life hasn't changed, but mine has. And I'm glad it has."

He took another drink, his eyes annoyed. "I should kill you for what you did—"

"But you won't, so shut up about it." I dropped onto one of the couches, my arms on my knees.

Bartholomew stilled at my words, the rim of the glass in his fingertips. Silence passed, as well as a cloud of anger and lightning storm of rage. He grabbed the bottle by the neck and carried it over before placing it on the coffee table between us. "You should have just given her up. Now your neck is on the line."

"He can't kill me."

"He's killed lots of people—I'm sure he can."

"I hope he tries. Would give me the opportunity you've denied me."

He stripped off his jacket and tossed it on the floor before he sat back. One ankle propped on the opposite knee as his arm rested over the back of the couch. He took a lazy scan of his living room as he sat there, the three glasses of scotch already making his eyes sag slightly. "I have a lot of shit on my plate right now, Benton. Don't have time for this bullshit."

"Then let me kill him."

"He's worthless if he's dead."

"Kill him and absorb his business."

He shook his head. "Too much work. Our current setup is lucrative enough. And I've got other plans."

"Like?"

He gave me a cold look. "I'm afraid if I tell you, you'll take his girl too."

"I have a girl."

He rolled his eyes. "How romantic…"

"What is it?"

He grabbed the glass off the table and poured another drink. Instead of taking a sip right away, he raised it slightly, as if making a toast. "The Skull King."

As if his words were concrete, they crashed to the floor with a heavy thump. "You want to be his distributor?"

He readopted his relaxed posture, getting comfortable on the couch. "No."

"You want him to be our distributor?"

"No."

I shook my head. "This better not be going where I think it's going."

"It is."

"That's fucking suicide."

He gave a shrug. "It'll be fine."

"Taking over the cult is too much work, but you think this is a walk in the park?"

He took a drink. "You know how much cash he's bagging? A lot more than us."

I shook my head in disbelief.

"We take France and Italy, and we'll be the biggest kingpins—"

"There's no *we* in this, Bartholomew."

He was about to take a drink but steadied his glass instead. He gave me a hard look, full of ominous threat, and then sat forward again. His glass returned to the table, and he stared at me with a look that was borderline demonic. "Let's not forget, I own you—"

"He'll kill us all."

"There's always going to be causalities—"

"Maybe you don't have something to live for, but I do. I'm out."

"You don't have a choice—"

"You bet your ass I do. Our rule is unchallenged here in France, but it's a different situation across the border. He owns Florence with the same iron fist that we own Paris. This isn't a simple conquest. This is a war that could go on for decades, that could cause a blood feud that will last generations. Not. Worth. It."

After everything I said, his only response was a shrug.

"I'm not just saying this selfishly. I'm saying it for your benefit too. It will cost your life."

He gave another shrug.

"Bartholomew."

With a bored look, he regarded me.

"Look at everything we've accomplished here. And we still have so much to do."

He suddenly gave me a smirk.

"What?"

He took another drink. "You said we."

BY THE TIME I got home, it was nearly noon.

I was approaching the steps when my phone vibrated with a text.

I pulled it out and saw the message from Constance. *Are you alright?*

I was almost to the house, but I replied anyway. *Yes. Will you be home soon?*

I shoved the phone back into my pocket and walked through the front door.

She came into the entryway the second she heard me enter. She gave me a quick look-over, as if she expected me to be covered in blood, then seemed relieved to see I was returning in the same condition as when I left. She immediately moved into me and embraced me with a hug, one arm hooking around my neck while the other hugged my waist. Her little body gave a gentle thud against mine before she latched on.

My response was automatic at this point, and my arms circled her petite frame and drew her close. My chin rested on her head as I squeezed her beautiful body against mine, my fingers digging into the fabric of her shirt. She smelled like fresh roses in summer. Her hair was soft just like Claire's. Claire used to be the only thing I looked forward to whenever I came home, but now Constance was a close second.

She rose on her tiptoes and cupped my face as she kissed me. Her lips were hungry and had a distinct taste of scotch, like she'd had a glass with her breakfast this morning as she shook off the nerves.

My hand moved over her ass, and I squeezed it as I deepened the kiss, instantly falling into the heat we created together. It was like walking through fire.

She seemed to like it because her hands slid underneath my shirt and moved up my chest. She planted her palms against my pecs as she gave me her tongue, as she wore her need on her sleeve with desperation.

I liked her desperation.

This woman had survived a cult and killed a man to do it, but she still needed me anyway.

I got her into bed, our clothes off and our naked skin in contact. She was underneath me on the bed, and I sank deep as I looked into her eyes. This was the only way I'd taken her, and while I wanted to stare at her ass while I fucked her and shove her face into the mattress, this was the position I always found myself in.

I liked it.

I liked watching her eyes light up like beacons from a lighthouse.

I liked watching the tears pour from the corners of her eyes when she came.

I liked watching her take my big dick and beg for more.

With my arms pinned behind her knees, I took her hard and fast, slamming the headboard against the wall because there was no one else in the house to hear it. We glistened with sweat. We panted like animals. We came with loud grunts as we finished.

Then we lay there—all our pent-up stress released.

Once the heat passed, she snuggled into my side, her fingertips cold as if the short separation was enough to turn her to ice again.

I ran hot, so I relished her touch.

With her head on my shoulder and her hand on my stomach, she spoke. "What happened?"

I turned to lean my head against hers, her hair against my cheek and in the crook of my neck. "Told him to stay off my property."

"And?"

"That's it."

She lay still for a moment before she propped herself up on one elbow and looked down at me. Her hair was a curtain behind her, and her makeup was smeared from the sweat and the tears. "Benton."

"I left nothing out."

"And he just…accepted that?"

"He doesn't have a choice."

"So, you really think that's the end of it? That he'll leave us alone?"

I couldn't lie to her. As much as I wanted to make her feel better, I didn't want her to drop her guard. "He still wants you."

The light left her eyes—and it was a punch to the stomach.

"He might keep his eye on you, but he won't come near you or come into the house while we're away. No reason to be afraid."

She gave a sigh and lay down again, snuggling closer to me this time. "As long as he didn't make any other threats…I guess I can live with that."

ELEVEN

Constance

I'D JUST PULLED THE PAN OUT OF THE OVEN WHEN THE doorbell rang.

"Who's that?" Claire asked, looking up from her homework at the dining table.

Benton sat in the living room, paying bills and doing paperwork in just his sweatpants in front of the fire. "Uncle Bleu."

"Uncle Bleu?" Claire asked. "I'll have to introduce him to Bleu!" She slid off the chair and ran off.

He got to his feet and crossed the living room like a Roman soldier, his muscles his armor, his strength his weapon. The pants were low on his waist, so the vein that ran from below his belly button and underneath the fabric was visible—and sexy. Unaware of my stare, he walked out of the room and disappeared into the foyer.

He let his brother inside, exchanged a few words, and then appeared in my view.

Bleu looked at me and gave me a nod. "Hey."

"Hey," I said back, not sure what else to say because I really didn't know him. "Are you staying for dinner?"

"I hope so since I'm watching Claire tonight."

"You are?" Claire held up her bear to him. "Guess what I named him?"

He took it and looked him over, as if there would be a tag somewhere. "Grizzly?"

"No," Claire said. "Bleu!"

Benton clapped him on the shoulder. "Spitting image, huh?"

His brother flashed him a glare.

Benton hadn't told me about these plans, and I wasn't even sure why he needed Bleu at all. If he needed to leave the house, we were fine on our own. "Are you going somewhere?" My attention was turned to Benton, who stood there looking hard as rock.

Bleu took Claire back to the dining table and asked her about her homework. They fell into conversation, oblivious to us standing near the kitchen.

Benton held my gaze for a while before he cracked a faint smile. "*We're* going somewhere."

"We…?"

"I'm taking you to dinner."

"What?" The outburst exploded on its own because I was so surprised. "Really?"

"Yes."

"You?"

His eyebrows raised.

"I just… It doesn't seem like your thing."

"It's not."

"Well, don't do it just for me—"

"We doing this or not?"

I gave a nod. "Sure…I'd love to."

WE WALKED TOGETHER on the sidewalk, side by side, me wrapped up in a coat and scarf while he wore a long-sleeved shirt like it was a cozy sweater. He was in dark jeans that hung low on his hips, his muscled thighs stretching the denim. If there were a photographer in front of us, Benton would look like a model doing a shoot right there on the sidewalk.

"This is weird."

He gave me a side glance.

"I think it's the first time we've been out of the house without Claire…except when we drop her off at school in the morning."

"Bleu will take care of her."

"I'm not worried about that. It's just…different."

We stopped at the corner then crossed the street. There was a little bistro there, a nice place but not too nice.

"You know…" I stopped on the sidewalk before we could reach the hostess podium.

He turned back to me, his powerful arms by his sides, his blue eyes digging deep into mine.

"I'm happy just checking into a hotel room for a couple of hours…" Our relationship was anything but normal, so I didn't need to sit in a restaurant and have a date like a normal couple who'd met at a bar or something. Our circumstances set us apart from everyone else. What we had was deeper than any conversation we could have over a bottle of wine and candlelight.

His stare lingered on my face for a while as he considered it. "You don't want to have dinner with me?"

"That's not what I said—"

"But that's how it seems." His hard eyes pierced me like he was the hammer and I was the nails. "Why?"

"It's not that I don't want to—"

"Why?"

I glanced behind him, seeing the couples talking quietly with one another, the sounds of the guitar coming from inside the restaurant. "This isn't us…"

He pressed me with his look, wanting more.

"We aren't some couple that met each other online. Met in a bar. Whatever. And it's fine that it's not us. What we have…is deeper than a first date. There's already so much between us. I know this isn't your thing, and it's not my thing either."

"You didn't use to go on dates before all of this happened?"

"Yes. But that was before…and now I have you."

His hands slid into his pockets as he remained in front of me.

"I hope I never have to go on a date again…" I didn't realize what I said until it was out in the open between us. It just came out, pure honesty, feelings so raw they ached. It shouldn't have been said, but it was done now, and I had no idea how he would react.

He didn't react at all.

Now I couldn't take it back. It was just floating in the air between us, hanging there like a corpse on a noose.

He stepped closer, his eyes focused on mine as he drew near. He stopped just in front of me, his eyes dropping to my lips. One of his massive arms circled my lower back, and he tugged me into him before he laid a hot kiss on my mouth. "Let's go."

IT WAS a beautiful suite at a boutique hotel just a few blocks from his apartment. A four-poster bed, with white wooden dressers against the wall. The sheets were French linens, soft to the touch but also durable. Small pots of fresh flowers were everywhere, making it feel like summer instead of bitter winter.

He got me in the center of the bed, his heavy body directly on top of me, the heat from his skin traveling through the air and reaching my bare skin. Before he got his clothes off and came close, I was cold, lying on chilled sheets with pointed nipples. But once his hips were between my thighs and he smothered me against the mattress, he brought the summer sun into the wintry room.

His blue eyes took me in as he guided himself inside me, his head coated in my arousal so the entry was easy, flawless. He pushed through the initial tightness and sank deeper, invading all of me like a conqueror who already knew the lay of the land. He was a quiet lover, but his eyes were loud, and now they tightened in pleasure once he was fully inside me.

I was the opposite. I was full of gasps and moans, loud tears and sharp nails.

Once he got going, everything else faded from existence.

Forneus wasn't following me. The camp never existed. I didn't kill a faceless man with a knife. Beatrice wasn't mutilated like an animal. None of that happened. He made everything go away every time he touched me, every time he was buried deep inside me.

He took me once and kept going, still hard despite his release. Nothing could deter him. No amount of pleasure could make his satisfaction permanent. His hand slid into my hair and fisted it as he angled my hips farther, hitting me at a deeper angle than before.

I pulled him close and panted in his face, giving a mixture of whimpers and moans, of writhing nails that sliced into his skin, of gentle whispers of his name. "Benton…" He took me higher than I'd ever been, became a greater drug than the acid I'd been forced to take. It was therapeutic. It was healing. Cleansing.

I wondered if it felt the same for him.

BENTON OPENED the door in just his boxers and took the room service tray.

The woman couldn't hide her shock at his appearance, even though she probably saw this sort of thing often. But she'd never seen a man like Benton—a freakin' tank.

As he signed the tab, her eyes darted to me where I lay on the bed in a robe.

She sent me subtle thumbs-up.

I gave a quiet chuckle.

Benton didn't seem to notice—or more likely, didn't care—and brought the tray inside. He set it at the small dining table near the window and took a seat. He pulled the silver lids off the platters and got set to eat as if he wasn't going to wait for me.

I took a seat beside him and started to eat.

He'd ordered steak frites with a side of Brussels sprouts, then looked down at my dinner. He didn't say anything, but there was a subtle look of disapproval in his eyes.

"Breakfast is my favorite meal of the day."

He cut into his steak and ate, arms on the table, his eyes on me most of the time, and when they weren't, they were on his food.

He never made small talk. He never filled the silence with insincerity. Situations that were uncomfortable to regular people didn't make him uncomfortable at all. And he could say so much with just his expression that he didn't need his words much. I loved all of that. When I thought about the dates I'd had in the past, all the questions, getting to know each other, what we do for a living…tedious.

It was never tedious with him.

"You like your steak?"

He nodded and grunted at the same time.

I smiled as I took another bite of my chocolate chip pancakes, which were coated in syrup and whipped cream, a lot more delicious than his piece of meat.

He always inhaled his food the second he got it, so he was done much quicker. He'd ordered a bottle of wine, so he drank that as he watched me take my time with my potatoes and omelet.

"How do you think they're doing?"

"I'm sure Claire has introduced him to all her favorite ponies and invited her bear to join them for dinner."

I chuckled because that was probably exactly what had happened. "She's done that to you?"

"I've attended many tea parties for her guests."

"That's cute." He was impossible to place in a setting like that, but I could picture it because I'd witnessed firsthand what kind of father he was. There was nothing he wouldn't do for his daughter. "What was she like as a baby?"

"Easy but codependent."

"Meaning?"

"If I wasn't in the room, a tantrum would ensue."

"So how did you juggle work and childcare?"

"I didn't." He sat forward slightly, his bulging arms on display for me to admire. "Took a year off work."

"Beatrice wasn't involved?"

"Barely. Any time she'd try, Claire would sob and sob…"

"Because she wanted you." My heart melted into a puddle on the floor, picturing this gorgeous man being everything to that little girl.

His blue eyes held my gaze.

"Being a single father, that must have been hard for you."

After a long stare, he gave a shake of his head. "No."

"You went from bachelorhood and the criminal underworld to full-time father…that had to be rough."

"No." He didn't change his answer. He didn't change his attitude either. "They say mothers have maternal instincts that just kick in when they have their children. Same applies to fathers. She was born—and I just knew what to do. Having her was a huge disruption in my life, and while that was a challenge, it didn't bother me either. The rewards of parenthood far outweigh the sacrifices."

"Would you want more children someday?" I cut into the pancakes with the side of my fork then spun it in the pool of syrup. I didn't realize the implications of the question until it was already asked, and now I had to ride it out. I kept my gaze down for a while so I wouldn't have to see his reaction, but when the silence lingered for too long, I forced myself to look up.

"No."

My fingers kept spinning the fork even though I had plenty of syrup.

"Just me, no. But with you, yes."

My hold on the utensil slipped—and it clanked against the plate when it fell.

"If that's what you're really asking."

"Actually, I wasn't…" I picked up the fork again, but now I'd lost my appetite. "I was just…curious."

He watched me for a while, his blue eyes like microscopes. "Do you want to have children?"

"I always have. But now…I'm not so sure."

His eyes shifted back and forth.

"I love Claire like my own. So, I guess I don't really feel the need like I used to."

I'd said a lot of incredible things that night, but not once did he snap or distance himself. He took everything I said like a man—head on. It was hard to remember his coldness, even though it wasn't so long ago. Now he let me in, when he'd done everything he could to block me out.

"Are you still using me?"

The room went silent, and the air suddenly felt too thick to enter my lungs. My eyes stopped in place, like his gaze was a searchlight that made me freeze.

When he didn't get an answer, he asked a different question. "If Forneus were dead, would you still be here? That's what I'm asking."

I gave a nod. "As long as you still wanted me here…"

He studied my face a moment longer. "I would."

I drew a deep breath, seeing the sincerity in his beautiful eyes.

"And whether you want to have children or you don't makes no difference to me."

I suddenly had a flashback. Backstage at the theater, I'd just danced my feet bloody, and he came walking through, holding up a picture to every person he encountered. His crystal-blue eyes met mine, desperate but calm, and I never forgot that look. I'd had no idea what would happen after that meeting, and I never expected to be sitting there with him now, talking about such things. And I certainly didn't expect this man to become my everything. My man. My home. My family. "I thought you weren't looking for that kind of relationship."

"I wasn't. Still not."

"Then why do you talk about us like it's forever?"

After a hard stare, he gave a subtle shrug. "Because we are."

I didn't know what that meant because some of his words were contradictory.

"I don't love you now. But I know I will. I don't want to get married. But I know that'll happen too. If something is right, I'm not going to push it away. There's only one woman I could ever be with—and she's you."

It wasn't a declaration of love. There wasn't a ring on the table. But it was somehow the most perfect thing he ever could have said. It was our story, a story that was different from everyone else's, a story that only made sense for us. Even if I could change the past and end up with a man who brought me flowers and dropped down to one knee…I would still want this instead.

THE HOUSE WAS A MESS.

All of her stuffed animals had vacated her room, and they were littered all over the couches. Her bear wore a crown in the armchair, like he was a prince on a throne, and Bleu sat on the floor with a paper crown on his head.

Bleu stilled when he heard us behind him—red in the face from embarrassment.

"Daddy, we're pretending to be princesses." Claire ran straight into Benton's arms like we'd been gone a lot longer than a couple hours.

Benton lifted her effortlessly and swiped a kiss across her forehead. "I see that. And Uncle Bleu is the most beautiful princess I've ever seen."

"Hey," Claire said. "What about me?"

"Second to you, sweetheart." He put her down again.

Claire took my hand. "Want to play?"

"Sure," I said. "But only if I get to be the queen."

"Ooh! You can be the wicked queen." Claire grabbed another paper crown and handed it to me.

I put it upon my head and took a seat next to one of her ponies. "Yes…I can be quite wicked."

Bleu tore off his crown and got to his feet. "You guys were out for a long time." He gave his brother a look of accusation. "A *very* long time."

Benton clapped him on the shoulder. "Thanks for watching her."

"I better get paid next time." Bleu gave Claire a hug goodbye, gave me a wave, and then left the apartment.

"Dad, here's yours." Claire handed him the paper crown. "You can be the king."

He placed it on his head and took a seat in one of the armchairs, looking regal in just his long-sleeved shirt and jeans. One ankle rested on the opposite knee, and he propped his elbow on the couch. "Alright. Now for my first order of business…"

TWELVE

Benton

Constance followed me to the door, the same sadness in her eyes as every other night when I left. They were dark like a glass of red wine, but so seductive in appearance. It made me want to stay—just for her.

She never liked to touch me over my clothing. Her palms always slid underneath my shirt and up the grooves of my abs until she reached my concrete chest. Her body came close, and she rose on her tiptoes to kiss me goodbye.

She devoured my mouth as if I hadn't just made her writhe in my bed only a few minutes ago. She gave me tongue. Gave me heat. Gave me fire. Her long nails gently scratched my skin as they made their way down to my abs again.

The second Claire wasn't in the room, Constance was all over me.

Always.

I broke apart first and looked at her parted lips, her

small tongue pressed against her bottom teeth, the sexy plea in her eyes.

Our goodbyes were always wordless. An exchange of physical affection. An exchange of heated looks. I loved that she didn't need to talk to get her point across, that she could do it with her lips and every other part of her body.

Her nails withdrew, and she reluctantly let me go.

But her eyes looked heartbroken.

My hand dug into her hair, and I gave her one more kiss before I walked out.

At the curb was the blacked-out SUV, the exhaust blowing, the engine quiet on the abandoned street. I got into the back, and we took off. "What's happening?"

"Dinner party."

I turned to meet his gaze.

"Remember Kline Weatherton?"

I gave a nod.

"He came through. We're seeing Carlyle."

"And what do you need me for? To kill him?"

"If I want someone dead, I'll kill them myself."

"Kline said you burned a bridge. What'd you do?"

He gave a subtle shake of his head. "It's just business. Sometimes people forget that."

"And what's my business tonight?"

"To do what I tell you."

My eyes narrowed as I stared.

He met my look, unapologetic.

I opened the door even though we were driving right through a green light and prepared to jump out.

"Alright." He grabbed my arm and yanked me back. "Poor choice of words…"

"You wouldn't have brought me in unless you needed me, so stop acting like you don't." I slammed the door shut and strapped on my safety belt again.

"Just follow my lead, alright? And don't shoot anybody."

"I have half a mind to shoot you right now…"

He gave a smirk. "I'd shoot you right back, and we'd both be dead. Kinda sweet, isn't it?"

We spent the next fifteen minutes in silence and approached an estate protected by an iron gate. The security guard let us pass through, and we pulled around the fountain to the front of the house. There was a statue lit up with floodlights, a soldier on a stallion.

We were met by the butler and entered the estate. Typical French architecture. Gold ceilings, textured mirrors, hints of rose gold in accent pieces, colorful rugs that looked like watercolor paintings.

We emerged in the sitting room, Kline sitting in an armchair with a glass of wine in his hand. A woman different from the one on his arm at the silent auction was propped on the armrest, her arm around his shoulders in a false display of affection.

Carlyle took one look at Bartholomew—and that set the tone for the night. He turned back to Kline, his eyes packed with an accusation of betrayal.

Kline looked away, too ashamed to meet that angry stare. "I was coerced—"

"And I'm insulted." He set down his glass and rose to his feet. "To be in the same room as this swine is beneath me. Let him linger too long, and it'll smell like a pigsty."

I lowered my voice. "What the fuck did you do?"

Bartholomew moved in his way, keeping him from the foyer. "Surely, you must be over this by now—"

"Shut your fucking mouth before I turn you into crispy bacon on Christmas morning."

The two men faced off, standing at the same height, but while Carlyle looked red and furious, Bartholomew looked like this confrontation was inconsequential.

If Bartholomew had brought me here to fix his mess, that wasn't going to happen. I wasn't even sure what provoked the problem. Carlyle was a diplomat by day, but he had deep ties into the drug trade, could get things done above and underground. So, it wasn't smart to piss him off.

"Your personal vendetta is irrelevant to our business relationship—"

"You slept with my *wife*."

I tried to keep a straight face, but the cringe came.

"There is no business relationship, Bartholomew. Not with you." Carlyle stepped around him and headed for the foyer. "I made it very clear you're no longer a partner in the game." He continued past me and headed for the front door.

Bartholomew narrowed his eyes on my face then gave a nod in his direction.

My eyebrows furrowed.

He did it again—this time with more purpose.

I rolled my eyes and went after him. I stepped into the cool night air and watched him approach his Bentley. "Carlyle."

He grabbed the door handle to his car and opened it. "I don't have time for this."

I shoved my palm hard against it. "I don't either, but I always have time to make more money." With my body against the car, he didn't reach for the handle again. It was impossible—because I was the size of an ox. "Let's do that together. Cut him out and work directly with me."

His hands slid into his pockets, and he stepped away slightly. Every breath he exhaled came out as smoke in the foggy air. "Didn't realize you were back in the game."

"Unfortunately."

"Why is that?"

"I'd rather be home with my family."

"And that son of a bitch got you mixed up in this shit again?"

I gave a shrug. "He did me a favor. Now I'm paying him back."

"Must have been a pretty big favor…"

"He saved my daughter's life."

He stilled at the announcement, his head cocked slightly.

"You don't have to deal with Bartholomew. You can deal with me instead."

He shook his head. "He'd still be benefiting."

"So would you."

He pulled a cigar out of his pocket, lit it, and then took a puff. When the smoke appeared, it immediately blended into the fog around us, the blanket of clouds that fell to the surface when the temperature dropped overnight. "I should kill him."

"But you can't—otherwise, you would have done it already."

He took another puff, his eyes hostile now.

"Let's not pretend that you don't have a different mistress on your arm every time I see you. That you aren't the first one in line at the whorehouses. Shit happens."

"You don't fuck your partner's wife."

"Doesn't seem like your wife means much to you, so maybe he assumed you wouldn't care."

"Doesn't matter—"

"It's in the past now. I've given you an agreeable solution, so let's move forward."

He enjoyed his cigar for another moment before he tapped the ash off the tip. "You want my advice?"

"Didn't ask for it."

He stepped closer, as if Bartholomew were right behind him. "Kill him. Then take everything for yourself."

"I told you he saved my daughter's life—"

"It's in the past now, right?" He threw the cigar on the ground and let the ash glow bright red. "He's not someone you can trust—and you better not trust him either."

THE SECOND we were in the back seat, he fired off his questions.

"What happened?"

"You fucked his wife, Bartholomew." I cast him a glare. "That's what happened."

He crossed one ankle on the opposite knee, propped one elbow on the armrest, and looked bored. "She walked right up to me and asked me to fuck her in the ass. What was I supposed to do? Walk away?"

I rubbed my temple as I kept my eyes straight ahead.

"Like you would have done anything different, asshole."

"I would have."

"Because your dick is a pussy."

"You could pay for any whore you want. But you still went for his wife? Still risked everything for a piece of ass?"

He gave a shrug. "That's exactly why, and I don't feel bad about it."

"Jesus…"

"So, what did he say?"

"You mean, did I fix your mess?"

He stared, hard and cold.

"Yes. I fixed your mess."

"So, we're back on the books?"

"I'm back on the books. He wants nothing to do with you."

His stare remained steady, as if he wasn't the least bit surprised. "Problem solved."

"Was that your plan all along?"

"You know me…I don't make plans."

"A heads-up would have been nice."

"But that made the conversation spontaneous. Organic. Real. And that's exactly what I wanted."

IT WAS one of the rare times I was home before Claire left for school.

And when she looked so damn excited, it made me feel like shit. She ran into my arms, asked me to make crepes even though Constance had already made breakfast, and it made me miss our old lives.

We'd had a great routine. We'd have breakfast together, I'd drop her off at school, and then I'd head off to work. We were both out of the house at the same time, so we were home at the same time too.

Now, seeing her in the morning was a luxury, and I was asleep when she got out of school most of the time.

We sat at the table and had breakfast together, and when she was done, we both walked her to school. It was a cold morning, but there were no signs of rain, and when March arrived, the sky would be blue.

I looked forward to the summer, when she was out of school for months and we were at the estate in the countryside. We'd take care of the horses, go swimming, and spend quality time together. I usually took the summers off from construction so I could spend all my time with her.

That was over too.

I hugged her goodbye and watched her run off to be with her friends.

Constance and I walked back.

"How was your night?"

I hadn't said a word to her since I came home. My entire focus was on my daughter, and I'd forgotten she was there, to be honest. "Bullshit—like always."

She was in a gray pea coat with black jeans and boots. With every step she took, there was a tap against the sidewalk, more taps than I made because one step of mine was equivalent to two of hers.

"Are you ever going to tell me exactly what you do?"

"You really want to know?"

"Yes."

"Because you aren't going to like it."

"After being at the cult for so many months, I don't think there's anything you could say that would disturb me."

"But you may not like the kind of man I am."

She kept my pace, her eyes on the sidewalk in front of us. "There's nothing you could say to change the way I feel about you."

I believed her. I could hear it in her voice. Being on the streets granted me a level of intuition that nobody else had. I could read any room I stepped into. I could understand any person just by looking at them. I could tell if someone was lying just by listening to their tone.

She never lied to me—not once. "Drugs. Blackmail. Prostitution. Murder."

"That's what I figured."

"And that doesn't bother you?"

"I know that's not who you are anymore."

"But that's exactly who I was before Claire. If she'd never been born, nothing would have changed."

"But it did change, and that's all that matters."

I gave her a side glance. "I don't think another woman would be so accepting."

"I'm not scared—not when I know you can protect me."

My stare on the side of her face lingered. A rush of warmth flooded me, a mixture of desire, egotism, and a lot of other things. People were exiled from my life, so they never had the opportunity to know me—but she knew me better than anyone. She was the one raising my daughter with me. She was the one who protected my daughter when I couldn't. She was the only person who understood exactly what both of us had been through.

The second we walked in the door, the exhaustion hit me. The excitement I'd felt at catching Claire before school quickly faded once I was in the quiet apartment. I headed for the scotch in the living room and took a drink without pouring a glass.

Hands ran up my back before they slid underneath my shirt. Warm lips pressed against my skin. Nails dragged over my abs. Her jacket and blouse dropped, and then her hard nipples pressed against my bare skin.

I took another drink before I set the bottle down. "We'll do this when I wake up." I turned back around, sliding through her fingertips, and looked down at the woman who wanted to sink her claws into me the second I walked through the door.

"No." Her hands went to my jeans and got them undone.

I stood with my arms by my sides, listening to the echo of the word. Every time I heard it, it turned me on more. More and more.

She pushed my jeans to my knees then guided me back to the couch. When the backs of my knees hit the cushion, she gave me a gentle shove.

I fell back, my dick hard because I couldn't get that word out of my head.

No.

Everything below her waist was shed before she straddled my waist. She scooted close, her tits in my face, and then she lowered herself onto my length.

I closed my eyes as I gave a moan.

Fuck…this pussy.

Her hands clamped onto my shoulders like they were rungs on a ladder and moved up and down, rolling her hips at the perfect moment to catch more of my dick. Over and over, she undulated, nice and slow, like she was in no hurry to get off.

She just wanted to enjoy me.

Each one of my hands grabbed a cheek and squeezed as I pushed my hips up to thrust inside her.

Her hand flattened against my chest to steady me.

"Don't move." She said it in a sexy whisper, still riding me up and down. "You said you were tired, remember?" She flicked her hair to the side and kept her shoulders back, putting her perky tits on display right in front of me. "Allow me."

THIRTEEN

Constance

After I picked up Claire from school, we dropped by the market to grab some groceries. There was a little place close to the apartment, so it was easy to stop and get whatever I needed for dinner later that night. Benton rarely ordered out, and he preferred his meals to be comprised of fresh and organic options. That meant I had to go to the store nearly every day—not that I minded.

Claire grabbed a box of cookies off the shelf. "Ooh…"

"Put it back."

She gave me a smirk and threw it in the cart.

"Claire."

"Pleeaaasssseee."

"Your father said sweets are only for special occasions."

"But is Dad here…?" Her hands went behind her

back, and she squirmed in front of the shelves of packaged cookies and sweets.

I should put my foot down and say no, but it was hard to resist someone so sweet. "Fine…but this stays between us."

"Cross my heart…" She made an X over her chest. "Hope to die…" Then she pointed her fingers close to her face. "Stick a finger in my eye!"

I cocked my head. "What?"

She laughed like it was all a big joke and continued down the aisle.

After we paid for the groceries, we took a seat on the bench outside. I opened the box of cookies, and we enjoyed them together as we watched people walk up and down the sidewalk.

"Constance?"

"Yes, honey?"

"Are you and Daddy going to get married?"

I'd just taken a bite of the cookie, but it halted in my mouth for a moment. It took me a second to chew again, to break it down and into my throat. "Why do you ask?"

Her legs hung off the bench, so she kicked them and they swung like swings. "Because I saw you kissing…"

"You did?"

She nodded, a smirk on her face with a splash of rouge in her cheeks.

She was a little girl to me, but I forgot that she was smart and observant. I should have assumed she would figure it out eventually. But now that the moment had arrived, I didn't know how to handle it. "How does that make you feel?"

"What do you mean?"

"Would it be okay with you if we got married?"

She nodded enthusiastically.

"So, it's okay that I like your father?"

She nodded again. "I like him too."

"Well, is it okay that I kiss him?"

She laughed before she gave another nod.

"Good."

"Do you looooooovvvvvve him?" She leaned into me and nudged her shoulder into my arm, like we were two immature girlfriends discussing their crushes.

I leaned the box toward her so she could grab another cookie. "This stay between us, huh? Just like the cookies?"

She took another bite and chewed loudly before she gave a nod.

"Yes."

―――

DINNER WAS ROASTING in the oven while the sides were in the pots and pans on top of the stove. I'd never been much of a cook, but my new life had turned me into a chef. Claire didn't seem to mind it anymore, and I was quite proud of myself for all the progress I'd made. When it had been just me alone in my apartment, I might have thrown together a sandwich, but that was the extent of my abilities.

Benton emerged from the hallway, but he wasn't shirtless and barefoot anymore. He was in his jeans and a long-sleeved shirt—which meant only one thing.

"You're leaving?"

He walked up to me, intense blue eyes piercing me the second they made contact. It was always that way, like he could latch on to me without touching me. He never gave an answer—at least not a verbal one.

"We haven't even had dinner yet." Domestic bliss was shattered, and I turned into an angry wife who hated to watch her husband go. The only reason Claire and I were there was because of the sacrifice he'd made —but I didn't want him to pay the price anymore. I hated that he was gone most nights, and I slept alone in his bed, listening to every little sound in the house.

"I have a long night ahead of me."

I kept the protest locked away in my throat, but I was certain my eyes gave away my disappointment.

He talked to Claire for a bit before he said goodbye.

"Where are you going?" she asked.

He hesitated before he answered, as if speaking a lie was insufferable. "Work."

"I thought you builded things?"

"I do. It's a big project, so it needs to be done overnight. And it's *built*." He gave her a kiss on the forehead before he opened the cabinet and pulled out the garbage so he could take it out before he left. Before he tied the strings together, he stilled.

"What?" I asked.

He reached inside and pulled out the small box of cookies. His eyes immediately went to me, accusatory.

I was prepared to lie and say those were just for me, but Claire gave us away. "Uh oh…"

His eyes moved to hers before he tossed the box back into the garbage can. He tied the strings and lifted it to carry it into the garage. The door shut, and he was gone.

Claire immediately turned to me. "Daddy's gonna be mad…"

Benton returned and washed his hands in the sink.

I came to his side and leaned against the counter. "We were grocery shopping—"

"I didn't ask for an excuse, so don't give one." He patted his hands dry with the towel and didn't look at me. "She had way too many sweets over the holiday break, and if she's asking for sweets, especially before dinner, then she's had even more sweets than I realized."

"It was just a one-time thing—"

"Don't let it happen again." He tossed the towel on the counter and headed to the front door.

Claire kept her head down at the dining table, as if her father would somehow forget she was there.

I followed him to the front door. "Don't you think you're being a little harsh—"

"I haven't even raised my voice, so you've never seen me harsh." His eyes bored into mine, enraged.

My arms crossed over my chest, and I didn't back away. "It was just a spontaneous thing—"

"Did I ask for a list of excuses—"

"Don't interrupt me."

His jaw hardened as well as his eyes.

"I'm not feeding her sweets all the time, so calm the fuck down. I take good care of your daughter, so get off my ass. I've earned enough autonomy at this point that I can buy her a box of cookies whenever I feel like it, alright? I'm not sorry—but you should be. Talk to me like that again—"

He yanked me into him and crushed a kiss against my mouth. His arm squeezed my lower back as he tugged me hard, and then his hand moved to my ass and gave it a strong squeeze.

It was as if the fight had never happened. My fingers were in his hair, my tongue was in his mouth, his dick was hard against my stomach.

Then he abruptly walked out without saying a word.

I SAT across from Claire at the dining table, the platters of food between us. Benton was usually at the head of the table, but the seat was now vacant. I'd made Claire a plate, but she hadn't touched a single thing. She just sat there, her elbows on the table, her chin in a palm.

"Honey, why aren't you eating?"

She shrugged. "Not hungry."

The Catacombs

Maybe Benton was right. I shouldn't have given her those cookies after all. "You need to eat something, so at least take a few bites." I took a few bites of chicken and then the scalloped potatoes.

"It smells weird."

"I know I don't cook as well as your dad, but it's not that bad."

She pushed her plate away.

I'd never seen her misbehave like this, act so defiant. My impulse was to berate her, to raise my voice the way Benton did until she complied, but I'd never struggled to get her to do anything before. I took a different approach. "Something on your mind?"

"Dad's mad at me." She kept her eyes down.

"Honey, he's not mad at you."

"I think so."

"I'm the one he's mad at. But…we resolved it."

Her eyes flicked up. "Yeah?"

I nodded. "Now eat."

She pulled the plate back toward her and grabbed her fork.

I took a few more bites and felt my stomach tighten suddenly. It was almost like a cramp but more intense. My fork was returned to the plate when I suddenly got a small hit of vertigo. It only lasted for a second. It came out of nowhere, and the only thing it reminded me of—

Claire got a piece of chicken on her fork and brought it to her mouth.

I knocked it out of her hand. "Don't eat that."

The fork clattered on the table, and bits of chicken got everywhere.

"Shit…no." I grabbed the edge of the table to steady myself because the room started to turn.

"Constance? What's wrong?"

I closed my eyes because the room wouldn't stop. "Don't eat the food…"

"Constance?"

I felt my body slide to the floor, felt my cheek hit the rug with a thud.

"Constance!" She crawled to me across the floor and gave me a shake.

My eyes opened, but I didn't see the chandelier above the table, the crown moldings along the ceiling, the dimmed lights. I saw decayed branches, moonlight through the trees, and then a face…

His face.

"Constance!"

"Claire…do as I say." It was the most powerful hit I'd ever taken because it was embedded in my food. I hadn't noticed it…probably because I was still used to it. My arms couldn't lift me off the floor—not for life or death. "Call Daddy…"

"I don't know how."

"My phone… It's on the table."

Her blurred form moved in my vision, a shadow in the tree line. She came back, her fingers hitting the screen to make it light up.

"The green button…in the corner." I closed my eyes, the demon's eyes looking into mine. Horns. Teeth.

Wings. There was nothing I could do but stare, watch the demonic grin. The trees caved in. The rain turned to hail. The hail turned to snow. I shivered as the water soaked into my skin…and then I started to drown.

"Daddy, Constance needs help…"

FOURTEEN

Benton

The door was unlocked when I arrived.

I drew my gun as I entered the house at a run. "Claire!"

"Daddy!"

I followed her voice to the dining room. Broken plates were on the floor, food tossed everywhere, and Claire was hiding underneath the table, her arms around her folded knees. When she saw me, she tried to crawl out.

"Claire, don't move." I did a sweep of the room and checked the hallway and the bedrooms downstairs. There was no sign of forced entry—and there was no sign of Constance either. I ran upstairs, searched that place high and low, and then I ran back downstairs. "Constance!"

I came back to the dining room, where Claire remained cowered under the table. My daughter was here, and I was relieved.

But my woman was gone, and I was fucking terrified. "Claire, what happened?" I yanked a chair away and helped her out. My hands ran over her arms and checked her for signs of injury. She was in the same condition as I left her, just with puffy cheeks from all the crying. "Where's Constance?"

"I don't know…" She could barely speak between her sobs. Her chest heaved and gasped for air.

"Tell me what happened." I grabbed her arms and kept her still. "Come on, sweetheart."

"I don't know… We were eating dinner…and then she fell."

"On the floor?"

She nodded. "It's just like…when they would make her take that stuff."

I knew who they were…and the stuff she referred to. My eyes darted to the food all over the floor—and I made the connection. "Claire, did you eat anything?"

She shook her head.

"Not a bite?"

She shook her head again. "She told me not to…"

"Has anyone been in the house?"

"No."

I got to my feet and left her on the rug. "Where's Constance?"

"I couldn't understand anything she said…she was just talking. And then she went around the house and kept making weird noises…and then she left."

Now I knew why the door was unlocked.

"Daddy…I'm scared."

The Catacombs

I pulled out my phone and made the call.

It took several rings for him to answer. "What do—"

"Shut up and listen. I need you at my house now. No questions asked." I hung up. "Claire, listen to me." I grabbed her arms again. "Uncle Bleu will be here any minute. You're going to wait right here—"

"Daddy, no. Don't leave me here."

I squeezed her arms. "Remember when Constance was brave for you?"

She stared, tears streaming down her cheeks.

"When she made everything better? When she made all the bad things disappear?"

She nodded.

"Be brave for her."

She cried a little longer before she gave a nod.

I gave her a quick kiss on the forehead then sprinted out the door.

At that exact moment, Bleu's truck drove right up the sidewalk at fifty miles an hour. He slammed on the brakes before he crashed into the building. He hopped out and sprinted around the truck.

I ran around the other side and took the wheel. "Get Claire."

No questions asked, Bleu disappeared into the house.

I took off up the road, scanning left and right for a woman running for her life.

I CALLED in my men to make a perimeter ten miles around my apartment. If we didn't find her on the streets, that meant Forneus had taken her when she couldn't put up a fight. But that would break the truce, and he'd be stupid to do that.

I kept driving, kept turning down small streets, looking for her in the dark.

Bartholomew called. "Why the fuck are you pulling my men—"

"Because Forneus drugged Constance, and now she's missing. And it's *our* men—asshole." I hung up and made a sharp turn down a street I'd already driven down twice. "Come on, baby. Where are you."

I got another call. "We think we found her. The alley behind La Chanteria."

"Got it." I hit the brakes and flipped around, almost hitting a couple cars in the process. They honked incessantly as I sped away. Police lights flashed in the streets as people called in my reckless driving, but whenever they got close enough to recognize my face, they veered off.

I parked right on the sidewalk and sprinted into the alleyway. "Constance!"

She was on the ground against the wall, arms to her chest, caked in mud, a river of blood running down her head. She mumbled to herself, her eyes dazed like she could fall asleep, but she was too high for her brain to turn off.

I kneeled in front of her. "Constance."

Her head turned so her eyes could take me in, and

her entire face drained of blood. Snow-white, she looked like nothing but skin and bone. She started to tremble before she tried to crawl away, pushing herself against a wall that wouldn't move.

"Constance, it's Benton."

"No…no…it's not real." She pulled her body away, dragging it across the dirty concrete where the homeless pissed and the rats feasted. "It's real…this is the real…"

I grabbed her by the arm and forced her up upright. "Come on—"

"Ahhhhh!" Her arms flailed as she tried to fight me off, tears streaking down her face, murder in her eyes. "Don't fucking touch me…don't fucking…" She landed on the ground again, but this time, she didn't get back up.

I kneeled over her, and as I drew close, she panted harder, trembled uncontrollably.

This time, I didn't touch her, just came into her line of sight. "Constance—"

"I'm not your angel…I'm not…please don't." She kept her arms in front of her, palms up, her only defense.

I'd kill that motherfucker. I swore it then and there. "Baby."

She immediately inhaled a deep breath.

I finally got through to her. "I'm here now."

"Benton…?" She closed her eyes, and more tears streamed down her face, trickled to the pavement below her.

"Yes."

She breathed harder and harder, keeping her eyes tightly closed.

"I'm real."

She nodded, her teeth clenched tightly together.

"I'm going to take care of you, okay?"

She nodded again.

I reached for her hand.

She grabbed on to me, squeezing my hand like it was a lifeline.

I got her to her feet then carried her back to the truck at the sidewalk.

Her arms locked around my neck, and she buried her face in the crook, still breathing hard as she held on to me for dear life. "This is real…"

"Yes."

THE ONLY REASON the acid didn't kill her was because her body had developed a tolerance to it. That dose to anyone else would have been fatal. I took her to our medical facility, where the doctor pumped her stomach and then gave her some meds to keep her asleep so she could sleep through the rest of the high.

I sat in the armchair at her bedside when I heard heavy footfalls outside the door. The front door had opened and shut minutes ago, and I suspected I already knew the identity of the arrival.

He stepped into the doorway, dressed in all black,

giving Constance a look of sheer boredom. It lingered for a long time before it shifted to me—still bored.

Listening to a heated conversation between Bartholomew and me wasn't a pleasant way to wake up, so I left her bedside and joined him in the sitting room on the other side of the house. It was still sometime in the middle of the night, the lampposts casting a glow through the drawn curtains.

He uncorked a bottle of wine sitting on the table, filled a glass, and took a drink, but he obviously didn't like it because he threw the entire glass into the burning fire in the hearth. It made a loud shatter, and the flames dwindled for a moment or two.

He dropped onto one of the couches, feet planted far apart, one arm on the armrest with his curled fingers underneath his chin.

I took a seat in the armchair and absorbed his stare.

His fingers rubbed against the coarse hair of his jaw. "Not to sound insensitive, even though I don't really care whether the girl lives or dies, but tonight has been one hell of a fuck show, and I don't like it."

"I don't like it either, Bartholomew."

"You shouldn't have pulled the men—"

"You shouldn't have let him live." If Constance had more than a few bites of her food, tonight could have ended much differently. Then nothing would stop me from cutting his throat to the bone. "I'm going to kill him—and you aren't going to stop me."

Bartholomew sat on the couch, his eyes still as if he

didn't believe a word I said. "Your memory seems to have crippled in old age, so let me remind you—"

"I haven't forgotten and I will always be thankful, but that was then, and this is now. I have a freak-show on my hands that's a threat to my family. He's not going to stop until I kill him—"

"Or until he gets his angel back—a much simpler solution."

"Not going to happen—"

"The plan was to get your daughter back and live happily ever after…or whatever bullshit way people describe it. It's not my fault you fucked up that pretty picture by bringing Constance into the mix. I'm not responsible for the events that have unfolded here, and I will not destroy a business relationship because of your stupidity."

My jaw clenched. "You said you would kill him—"

"If he broke the truce—and he still hasn't."

"You motherfucker—"

"You can keep adding these goddamn addendums, but it's not going to fix the problem. You know what will—"

"Killing him."

He closed his eyes in aggravation. "We go down that route, we open up a whole new mess of problems. He's got a lot of allies in the shadows, got a lot of money to throw at his problems, has a lot of crazy that would defeat our logic. I know you're worked up right now so you can't think straight, but you know I'm right."

I was tempted to grab that bottle and slam it over his head.

"He's expecting it, and if he's expecting it, then that means he's prepared. And if he's prepared, even if we win, we're going to lose men, resources, and our guard. Our enemies will take ample opportunity to hit us because we can't win two wars at once. You know I'm right."

My hands clenched tightly.

"I'm not willing to risk everything I've built—not even for you."

"I don't need your help, Bartholomew. I can do this alone—"

"Sure, you might be able to kill him. But what about everyone else? What about the other eleven demons that have lost their brethren? The others that are loyal to him—even beyond the grave? There is no scenario where you get everything you want, Benton. You go after him, and I tell Forneus you went against my wishes, because I'm going to protect my ass before I protect yours. Maybe if you hadn't broken your vow, things would be different…but they aren't."

All I could do was give a subtle shake of my head.

"There's only one option if you want this to end."

"I'm not giving her up."

He inhaled a deep breath then slowly let it out. "If this woman loves you and Claire as much as you love her, then she would do the right thing. She wouldn't put you two through this. She's using you for safety, and she'll let you destroy yourselves to protect her—"

"She's the only reason my daughter is still alive. She can use me all she wants—she's earned it."

He gave me another bored stare, as if I was just some idiot. "But is she worth Claire's life, Benton? Because that's what it's going to come down to…eventually."

"He doesn't care about Claire."

"But he knows you do."

FIFTEEN

Constance

When I opened my eyes, my vision was steady. The wallpaper had blush-colored roses on dark vines. The crown molding along the ceiling was a dull gold. The chandelier that hung over the bed was off, so the room was dark except for the faint light coming through the closed curtains.

My arms were tucked under the blankets, my fingertips against the sheets. I was flat on my back, and I wondered how long I'd been that way. The second I was conscious, I was aware that I had to pee, so I must have been out for some time.

A man's silhouette was in the chair beside me, enormous shoulders and strong arms on the wooden armrests of the chair. He was slumped over slightly, as if he'd fallen asleep at my bedside. I blinked several times before the picture became crisp, before my mind became sharp enough to understand my surroundings.

"Benton…?" My voice came out like sandpaper against a rock.

He stirred at the sound of my voice, his eyes opening and instantly clear. He took me in for a breath before he scooted to the edge of his seat and closer to my bed. His blue eyes were hard and pained, a bit broken.

My hand reached for his, and the second I gripped it, I was hit with the most relaxing feeling I'd ever known. Everything was better. All the aches that I'd noticed once I was conscious were gone.

The high was back—the good one.

My memory was blurry, and I couldn't piece together the events from the night before. I could hardly believe I was alive because the dose I ingested must have been lethal. The last coherent memory I possessed was collapsing at the dining table and asking Claire to call her father. She must have gotten through to him and he came to my rescue. "Claire? Is she—?"

"She's fine. With Bleu."

"She didn't eat any of it—"

He shook his head. "She's a little scared…but that's it."

"Oh…thank god."

His hand cocooned mine. Warmth radiated to my fingers like I'd been frozen a moment ago.

"What happened…?" My voice still broke, like I hadn't had water for days.

"When I came to the house, you were gone. You'd wandered the streets for a while. Finally found you in an alleyway. You were a little bloody from hitting your head, had scraped knees and a couple cuts on your arms, and were dirty from falling in puddles along your way. I got you to the doctor, and they pumped your stomach."

"Would I have died if you hadn't gotten to me?"

He shook his head. "The doctor said it was a fatal amount to anyone else—but you'd developed a big tolerance."

"I guess that makes sense…"

"Do you remember anything?"

I shook my head. "Just trees…the demon…images here and there."

"You didn't recognize me."

"Because I can't see when I'm like that…or at least, can't see with my eyes."

He dipped his head slightly, his eyes on the comforter.

"What?"

He gave a subtle shake of his head. "I can't believe you had to go through that…however many times."

I squeezed his hand.

He squeezed it back.

"Did…did he come into the house?"

"No."

"Then I don't understand—"

"He poisoned your food before you brought it home."

"How?"

"He poisoned all the meats and vegetables in the store. A lot of people got sick. Some died."

"Oh my god…" He really was a serial killer. A sociopath. A psycho. "That…makes me sick."

He stared at our joined hands.

"What are we going to do…?"

He never answered.

I studied his hard face, watched the way he stared at our joined hands. His thumb lightly brushed over my soft skin, petting me. Without blinking, he stared, as if his mind were somewhere outside the room.

I had been happy to be alive a moment ago—but no more. "Benton, we don't have a choice—"

"Don't say that again." His eyes rose, their depths packed with hostility.

"Innocent people died—"

"And I don't give a fuck if the Pope was one of them. That's not an option."

"It's not worth it—"

"You're family—so you're worth it."

My eyes started to water.

"I will take care of my family."

WHEN WE WALKED out the bedroom door, I felt weak, just like I had all those other times. It always took a couple days to bounce back, to feel like myself again. The effects of the drugs still weakened my system and dulled my abilities.

Benton was there, his arm around my waist, being the crutch I needed.

Claire and Bleu were in the living room when we walked in, but her stuffed animals weren't all over the couches like last time. There wasn't a tea set on the table. The TV was on, but it didn't seem like she wanted to watch it.

Her eyes settled on me—and it was the same look I'd received every time I'd returned to the cabin.

She left the floor and sprinted to me. "Constance!" She hit me right in the stomach as her arms latched around me.

Benton supported my back so I wouldn't topple over. "Easy, sweetheart."

Her face was smothered in my stomach. "Are you okay?"

My arms smothered her with the same ferocity, and I squatted down to the floor so we could embrace each other head on. I locked my arms around her and held her for a long time, my hand cupping the back of her head, taken back to memories I wanted to forget. "I'm okay, honey. Just a little tired. What about you?"

"I'm scared…"

"Don't be." I pulled away and cupped her cheeks. "I know that was scary, but I'm okay. Everything is okay."

"You ran out of the house…and I didn't know what to do."

"You did the right thing by staying home. That was exactly what you should have done." I squeezed her shoulders next and gave her my best smile. "You're so smart, honey. And you didn't eat any of the food exactly like I told you."

She nodded.

"Now that I'm home, let's do something fun. You want to make some cookies?"

She still looked upset, but she gave a nod.

"Great. How about chocolate chip with walnuts?"

She crinkled her nose. "I don't like walnuts."

"You don't?" I knew that, but I wanted to get her out of her funk. "I thought you loved them?"

"No," she said with a laugh. "I said I hated them."

"No, I'm pretty sure you said you loved them and couldn't get enough of them."

"No," she said with another laugh. "They're gross."

"Alright. Then just plain chocolate chips. Come on, give me a hand." I got to my feet and nodded toward the kitchen.

Now that she was in a better mood, she ran straight to the pantry to grab the ingredients.

I turned back to Benton, who sat on the couch with his brother. The two were in deep conversation, their voices too quiet to carry over to us across the room. Their heads were down, and two glasses of scotch were already on the coffee table.

———

IT'D BEEN a long day entertaining Claire, especially when all I wanted to do was lie in bed and rest, but by the time she went to bed, she was the same sweet and loving little girl that I wanted her to be. She was all smiles and chuckles. A beam of light in every room she stepped into.

"Thank you." Benton appeared in my way in the hallway. "I know pretending everything is normal is the last thing you want to do right now."

All I gave was a nod.

"Ready for bed?"

"Yeah."

Benton turned off the lights and made sure the house was locked up before he joined me in the bedroom.

I helped myself to one of his t-shirts and got between the sheets, happy to be back in my bed.

Benton stripped down to his boxers, looking like a living sculpture with muscles made of marble, and then joined me. The second he was beside me, the heat radiated to every corner of the mattress, like the heater had just kicked on when the thermostat was cranked up.

I snuggled right against him the second he was close, using his hard-as-rock shoulder as a pillow. My hand rested on his hard stomach, and I tucked my leg between his knees. It was my favorite way to sleep, wrapped around a bear.

He pressed a kiss to my forehead and left his lips there, his arm circling my waist and keeping me close.

The moment he kissed me, it was as if nothing had happened the night before, as if our lives together hadn't been disrupted by an attack. It was just the three of us living simple lives under the same roof, taking care of Claire during the day and then each other during the night.

His deep voice pierced the darkness. "We need to move." His lips moved against my forehead as he spoke, the coarse hair from his jaw scratching me.

I pulled away so I could look him in the eye. "What…?"

"You asked what we're going to do. I think that's what we should do."

"Move…but where?"

"Canada. A lot of people speak French there."

"You don't think he'd come after me there?"

"He might. But the pursuit will be a major inconvenience. He'll lose interest eventually. Here, it's too easy to keep tabs on you without disrupting his life."

"But Claire…she'll have to change schools."

"She'll make new friends."

"What about Bartholomew? I thought that was nonnegotiable."

His eyes dropped for a moment. "I'll talk to him."

"He's not going to change his mind—"

"Then I'll make him change his mind. If he's not going to help kill him, then this is the only other option."

I propped myself up on my elbow as I held his hard stare. "I…I don't want you to uproot your entire lives—"

"We stick together, baby. Period."

SIXTEEN

Benton

I STAYED HOME WITH HER FOR A COUPLE OF DAYS.

Bartholomew didn't like it, but he didn't dare say a damn word about it.

I took Claire to school in the morning, and in that snapshot of a moment, it felt the way it used to. When I was just a father and nothing else. My daughter was my entire world, and the cult didn't exist.

But when I came home, the reality set in.

Instead of going to my favorite market, I had to head somewhere new, twenty minutes out of the way so Forneus wouldn't be able to repeat his diabolical plan. He played by the rules, but like the snake that he was, he always found a loophole.

When lunch was ready, Constance came out of the bedroom, modeling my sweatpants and shirt. Despite how long she'd slept, she still had bags under her eyes, a discoloration to her skin that just wouldn't fade. Her gait wasn't the same, a lot slower, and she carried herself like a frail woman in a nursing home.

I couldn't even begin to imagine the internal destruction the acid had caused. Constance was a strong, no-excuses kind of woman—and it managed to defeat her.

She took a seat, gave me a smile, and then picked at her salad with her fork. "I like it when you cook. You're a lot better at it than I am."

"You've gotten better."

She chuckled as she kept her eyes on her food.

"What?"

"You don't sugarcoat things—I like that."

I watched her eat, watched her enjoy my company like I was charming and interesting, when I absolutely wasn't. "Most people don't like it. They just think I'm an asshole."

"Well, they don't get you." Her eyes remained down on her food, keeping the conversation casual. "I do."

Whenever I sat down to eat, food was my priority, and I scarfed it down as quickly as possible. It was a quality I'd picked up being a single father because there were few opportunities to eat in between the cries, the feedings, the blowouts. If you didn't eat as quickly as possible, it would grow cold, and you might not even get the opportunity to eat again for a couple hours. But now, I didn't eat. With my elbows on the table, I stared at her instead.

She finished a couple bites when she felt my stare. She raised her chin and met it head on, not intimidated like she used to be. The barrier I forced between us was long gone, and she quickly felt like Bleu or Bartholomew…before that went to shit. She was someone I trusted. She was someone I cared about. But she was also someone I wanted to fuck—and that was a first.

When I didn't say anything, she went back to eating.

As if I didn't need to say anything.

———

"WHERE'S CONSTANCE?" Claire sat across from me at the dining table.

"Asleep."

"Is she okay?"

"She's fine, sweetheart. Just tired." When I'd gone to grab Constance for dinner, she was asleep, so I'd let her be.

"I remember Mom used to be sleepy for days…" She pushed her food around with her fork, playing with it rather than eating it, which always ticked me off, but I wasn't in the mood to scold her right now.

"She'll feel better tomorrow."

"Okay. I miss her."

"She misses you too."

She finally started to eat, dipping her fork into a small amount of mashed potatoes before she got it into her mouth. "I like it when she picks me up from school."

"And you don't like it when I do?" I kept my tone

playful, but there was definitely a note of jealousy there. I'd never experienced jealousy in my life before, not for a woman, and not for Beatrice with Claire, but I felt a sharp intake of it now.

"No, I do. But she usually takes me shopping with her."

I liked to do all my errands while Claire was at school because it was much easier than taking a seven-year-old everywhere.

"She lets me pick things out. And then we talk and stuff…"

"What do you talk about?"

She shrugged as she pushed her potatoes around again.

"You can talk to me about anything, sweetheart."

"But we talk about girl stuff…"

"Girl stuff?" I asked, cracking a smile.

"Yep. Like boys…"

"You like a boy, Claire?"

"No!" She gave me her angry eyes. "Not me."

"Then Constance likes a boy?"

Now she grinned.

I knew who that boy was, and he wasn't a boy at all, but a man.

"She told me something…but I'm not supposed to tell you."

"Then you shouldn't tell me."

"I know, but it's hard…"

"If someone entrusts you with a secret, you should always keep it."

"Even from my daddy?"

"Well…in some cases."

"Is this one of those cases?" she asked.

"Depends. Is anyone hurt? Or in danger?"

She shook her head.

"Then no."

She dropped her head and looked at her food again. The fork swirled through her potatoes then she brushed it over her chicken like she was plastering a new construction.

I assumed the conversation was over.

She looked up at me and grinned.

I met her look as I chewed a bite.

"She said she loves you."

I chewed my bite as if nothing happened.

"Are you going to get married?"

I'd never imagined we'd have this conversation, that my daughter would interrogate me about my love life. I should be the one interrogating her. "Someday, maybe."

"So, you love her too?"

I took another bite.

"You can tell me. I won't tell her."

I chuckled. "I'm not falling for that."

"Dad, come on." She hit her palm against the table.

"That's between me and her, Claire."

She stuck out her tongue and grabbed her fork again.

I was in a playful mood—so I stuck out my tongue back.

THE RAIN PELTED the windows as we moved together in my bed, her lithe body underneath mine, her ankles locked together, her nails anchored into my flesh. We breathed in sync, swallowed each other's moans, rocked together just enough to work up a sweat. The headboard was close to tapping against the wall, but I was careful not to make contact. This had become our nighttime ritual, my body dominating hers against the sheets, slow and steady, keeping our inferno contained.

We both found our release, and then the high was over.

I didn't lie there for more than a minute before I got up and started to dress. If I lay there too long, I'd never leave.

Constance propped herself up on her elbow and watched me, the sadness in her eyes. She didn't ask the question because she already knew the answer. She was back to normal again, so she no longer needed my support. We had to go back to our old lives.

I pulled on my jeans and long-sleeved shirt before I tucked my gun into the back of my jeans.

When I was fully dressed, she got out of bed, her hourglass frame striking in the dim light from the lamp on my bedside. She had a narrow waist, a sexy belly button, and small but plump tits that ached for my kiss. But all that beauty disappeared underneath one of my t-shirts.

She walked me to the door and prepared to say

goodnight. Instead of pleading with her eyes, she just looked defeated, as if the fight to keep me there was hopeless.

"There's a gun in my top drawer. It's loaded."

She gave a nod.

I gave her a kiss goodbye and a grip around the waist before I walked into the wet night.

EARLY THE NEXT MORNING, we pulled through the gates, up the cobblestone path around the fountain full of lily pads, and approached the three-story estate that looked as if it had been ripped out of a book about French aristocracy.

Bartholomew hardly spoke to me.

The silence was mutual.

We came to a stop, and I looked at the double front doors. Sunrise was across the land, showing a blue sky because the rain clouds had passed. The road glistened from the downpour the night before. I'd been running around town all night while Constance slept through it all. "Why are we here?"

Bartholomew shut the door.

I swallowed my annoyance and joined him. "Answer my question."

"Because we need him—that's why."

"For what? He's been out of the game for years."

Bartholomew approached the door and used the

gold knocker to announce his presence. "You didn't always ask so many questions."

"Because I was informed."

He slid his hands into his pockets and waited, like our conversation was wrapped up with a neat bow.

A moment later, the door opened, and we were greeted by a butler in a tux. "Can I help you?"

"I have an appointment."

Like the good butler he was, he narrowed his eyes. "No, you don't."

I stared at Bartholomew.

"I've been unable to reach him, so there was no other alternative—"

"You were unable to reach him because he doesn't want to be reached." He started to shut the door.

Bartholomew stuck his foot against the door to bar it from closing. "Bitch, did you just interrupt me?"

The butler kept his hold on the door. "If you would so kindly remove your foot…"

"Tell him I'm here to see him."

The butler kept trying to slam the door on his foot.

Bartholomew wore military boots—so he didn't feel a thing.

I grabbed him by the elbow. "Come on, let's go—"

"Open the door." A deep voice emerged from behind the butler, a voice I recognized even though it'd been a really long time since the last time I'd heard it.

Bartholomew withdrew his foot and gave the butler a seething stare.

The butler stepped aside and revealed him

The Catacombs

standing bare-chested in just his sweatpants, covered in sweat like he'd been working out in his home gym, and he held a shotgun—which was aimed right at us.

The butler grinned.

Fender came forward, his gun still aimed, his stone-cold face set in a look of malice. "You talked your way through my guards."

Bartholomew didn't reach for his gun or look remotely concerned. "That's what I do."

He came closer, his heavy feet loud against the tile. "Now they'll be executed—because of you."

He gave a shrug. "A dime a dozen, right?"

When he was close to the door, he lowered the shotgun to his side. He took in Bartholomew's face, his dark eyes shifting back and forth as if he was reading words off a page. "You must have a death wish, coming to my residence."

"I tried to call—but it's been disconnected."

"You know damn well that I'm retired. There's no promise of fortune that'll bring me back into the game. Now get off my property before I pump these bullets into your chest."

"Not trying to bring you back," Bartholomew said. "Just need some advice. How about your butler here makes us a hot pot of coffee, and we'll discuss—"

"Hospitality is issued to guests—not intruders." He raised the gun and held it out to his butler, who took it without question and carried it away. "But because of our history, I will grant your request." He abruptly turned around and stepped into an entryway that led to another room.

I gave Bartholomew a stare. "That went well."

"We're here, aren't we?" He went first and wiped his muddy boots on the rug.

I looked at the pile of mud and shut the door behind me. "Like the butler doesn't hate you enough as it is…"

"He'll hate me more by the time I leave."

We stepped into Fender's office and found him sitting in one of the two sofas that faced each other. His butler had already gotten to work and had a pot of coffee and three mugs on the table.

Fender sat there, elbows on his knees, his seething stare shifting back and forth between the two of us.

In the tense silence, the butler placed a tray of morning pastries between us—even though none of us would eat them. He finally departed and gave us the room to converse.

Fender stared at me for a while. "What happened? You left far sooner than I did."

"It's a long story. My daughter was taken. Bartholomew agreed to help me get her back—in exchange for my servitude."

Fender flicked his gaze back to Bartholomew. "That was fucked up."

Bartholomew kept up his bored look. "He left out the part where he deserted me and everyone else."

I rolled my eyes.

Fender stared at us for a while longer before he sat back. "Ask your questions."

"Daddy!" A little boy ran through the door, maybe three years old, and headed right for Fender.

The look he gave his son was drastically different from the one he gave us. He actually smiled—and I'd never seen him smile. His arms were ready for the boy, and he scooped him up into his chest in one fluid motion. "My boy."

I remembered Claire at that age. I remembered every single moment of her short life.

Then his wife emerged, her stomach so big she looked as if she could give birth any day. She stilled when she saw us. "I…I didn't realize we had guests." Her eyes were filled with suspicion, as if she didn't like us one bit.

"They aren't guests." Fender got to his feet and carried his son back to his wife. "They'll be gone in a few minutes." He gave her a kiss as he placed one hand against her stomach, his son in one arm.

She gave a nod then took their son by the hand out of the room.

Fender returned, and as if that scene had never happened, he scowled. "That's what you're keeping me from. So be quick."

Bartholomew rubbed his hands together. "I'm taking on the Skull King."

Fender smiled again, but it was a different kind of smile than the one he showed before. It was sarcastic, incredulous. "Still ambitious…"

I didn't bother to voice my objection because I'd be living in Canada soon, not getting wrapped up in this idiocy.

"Yep. Any contacts, intelligence, and advice would be most appreciated."

"Acquiring my business wasn't enough?"

"If you'd stayed in the game, you would have made the same decision too. If the Skull King were removed, we could plant our own men there and acquire an entirely new line of business. If I want to scale up, I need to acquire more clients and more distributors. Makes the most logical sense."

Fender gave a chuckle, and it sounded strange coming from him, a man who never cracked a smile.

"What?" Bartholomew asked.

Fender shook his head. "You remind me of myself."

"Then I'll take that as a compliment."

"You shouldn't—because I was mad." Now he turned serious again. "You want my advice? Here it is. You already have everything. You know what everything plus more of everything equals? Everything. There's no difference, Bartholomew. Enrich your life with something else, perhaps a woman that your dick worships, gain immortality through your sons and daughters. This stupidity risks not only your business and your life, but your sanity. Gross wealth fixes a lot of problems, but it doesn't fix everything."

Bartholomew's face remained stony and steady, as if none of that meant a damn thing. "You know that's not the advice I want."

"Advice is objective," Fender said. "Not subjective."

"It's fine that you decided to settle down and play house, but that's not me. It'll never be me. I want everything plus more of everything, and if it claims my life in the process, so be it. I'd rather die in the prime of my life than live to an age where someone is paid to wipe my ass every day. That's your future—not mine."

Fender brought his hands together, his gaze hard.

"So, tell me what I need to know—for old time's sake."

WE STEPPED INTO THE HOUSE, the girls still there from yesterday.

"You know he's right." I followed Bartholomew as he went for the bar.

"Fender's lost his mind." He poured himself a glass then turned back to me. "Why else would he give up everything for a woman? Why would he give up an empire to change diapers and screw the same pussy every single day?"

"He didn't lose his mind. Just got bored."

Bartholomew laughed into his glass then fell into a chair. Right away, one of the girls came up behind him and started to rub his shoulders. "If you're bored, you ain't doing it right."

I took the other seat. "I'm out, Bartholomew."

"You're not out until I say you're out."

"Too bad—I'm done."

Once he realized I was serious, he swatted the woman away and leaned forward. His glass was set aside, and he fixed his sharp stare on my face.

"We either kill Forneus and I stay—or I take my family elsewhere."

All he did was give a subtle shake of his head.

"I'm not going to live my life with a freak lurking in the shadows behind me—not when I can't put a bullet between his eyes. Canada sounds like the right place for us to start over. It's far enough away that he'll have to decide which is more important—his obsession or his business."

"Based on the actions of you, Fender, and Forneus, I suspect he'll choose the woman—like an idiot."

"If he comes for us, then I will kill him."

He shook his head. "I don't approve of this—"

"I don't need you to. I appreciate what you did for my daughter—"

He was on his feet. "If it weren't for me, your daughter would be a sack of bones right now. She would have died from the acid or from the knife to her back—"

"Shut your fucking mouth." I was on my feet too, ready to slam my fist into his face and knock his lights out. The calm turned into rage, just the way a simmer turned into an inferno with just a sprinkle of gas. It ignited—and then burned white-hot.

"You had the audacity to come back here after what you did—and I still helped you."

"I'm forever grateful—"

"Then fucking show it."

"Let's kill the freak, and I will. It's him or me, Bartholomew. You can't have both. You can't expect me to leave my family every night, knowing he's out there looking for another loophole to exploit."

He grabbed his glass, finished the contents, and then smashed it on the floor. "I already told you the answer is no."

"Then I'm leaving."

He took a few steps before he turned back to me, his arms tense by his sides. His gaze was so hot it could weld metal. "You're not going anywhere. I own you, asshole. Fucking own you."

Something hit me in that moment. Must have been what he said…or the way he said it. An epiphany of some kind. Instead of walking into every meeting as an equal, I was kept in the dark. I had to learn everything on the go. Carlyle's words came back to me. *"He's not someone you can trust—and you better not trust him either."*

Bartholomew stared me down, breathing heavily, like he wanted to rip my face off.

When we'd left Kline's place, we'd had a conversation in the back seat. That came back to me too. *"I'm back on the books. He wants nothing to do with you."*

His stare remained steady, as if he wasn't the least bit surprised. "Problem solved."

"Was that your plan all along?"

"You know me…I don't make plans."

"A heads-up would have been nice."

"But that made the conversation spontaneous. Organic. Real. And that's exactly what I wanted."

It all hit me at once, like the ceiling of an old building finally tumbling down. It hit me everywhere—but I remained steady on my feet. I took one step. Then another. And then another.

His body pivoted toward me, as if he could sense the change in the air, the invisible tension that suffocated us both.

"I know why you won't move against Forneus."

"I already told you why—"

"Because that wasn't part of the deal."

His eyes narrowed.

"You needed me back to fix your mistakes, just like old times. But there was only one way to do that." I came closer.

He didn't move back, his arms tightening, his eyes focusing.

"There was only one way to get me back." I stopped just a foot away from him, our seething eyes locked on each other. "Claire."

Now he stepped back.

And that was when I knew. "Motherfucker." The hilt of the knife was in my hand one instant and then deep in his flesh the next.

He knew it was coming, but he let it happen. He gave a quiet wince when the knife was fully in his stomach.

I held on to the hilt—and twisted.

He refused to grimace, took it like a man.

I left it there, listened to the drops of blood drip to the tile floor. A stampede of heels sounded behind us as the girls hurried out of the room before the battle escalated.

He breathed a little harder but didn't remove the knife. "I deserved that."

I pulled out my gun and cocked it.

"But I don't deserve this."

"I think you do." I pressed the gun right between his eyes.

He didn't flinch. "They were never supposed to take Claire. Just Beatrice."

I lowered the gun, but it remained hot in my fingers.

"I may be heartless, but I'm not that heartless."

I was too angry to speak. All I could do was breathe. Feel my nostrils flare with every breath. I could feel the slight tremors in my body, the shakes before the earthquake. "You took the mother of my child?"

"Don't act like you give a shit about her."

"She's Claire's mother!"

"And I knew that would be enough reason. Because if it were anyone else, you wouldn't give a damn. And in the end, what does it really matter? Beatrice walked right out of your lives without looking back. She doesn't miss you, and you don't miss her."

"She didn't deserve what happened to her."

"And that was never supposed to happen. Forneus crossed me. He took Claire when he wasn't supposed to, and then he lied about having her when we went to retrieve her. The plan went to shit."

I shook my head. "I know you're a piece of shit, but this...this is low...even for you."

"It wasn't supposed to happen this way. I wouldn't lie to you—"

"You've done nothing but lie to me!" My fist slammed into his face, making him stumble back and lose his footing for a brief second. "You did all of this? Just to get me back? Because you fucked Carlyle's wife and couldn't get your shit together?"

The knife still protruded from his stomach, his shirt soaked with blood.

"All of this...because of you." I squeezed the handle of the gun, my finger inching closer to the trigger to put him down for good. "My daughter was in that horrible place...because of you. Beatrice is permanently scarred...because of you. Forneus is stalking me...because—"

"That one's all on you. And the reason all of this happened is because of *you*." He stepped closer to me, his nose bloody like his stomach. "You walked away from me. You abandoned me. You abandoned all of us. And, what? You thought that would be the end of it? You were all I had, Benton. You were the one guy that I trusted to watch my back. You were the only person in my circle. We weren't friends. We weren't associates. We were fucking brothers." Spit flew out of his mouth as his voice rose. "And you turned your back...and just left me there. You had Claire, and she became your family because of blood...but I thought we were family."

All I could do was shake my head. "You don't have children. You don't understand—"

"And you weren't supposed to have children, but you fucking did it anyway."

I would never issue an apology—not now or ever.

Bartholomew stared me down, his face slowly becoming paler and paler as the blood dripped to his feet. The rage was in his eyes, tight in the cords in his neck. "I'm sorry about Claire. Truly. That was never supposed to happen, and you know I would never fuck with her. But the rest of it…I'm not sorry. Because you're here—where you're supposed to be. I don't just need you, Benton. I…fucking miss you."

I stepped away and stuffed the gun into the back of my jeans. "I never want to see you again…if you live."

SEVENTEEN

Constance

I'D TEXTED HIM SEVERAL TIMES—NO RESPONSE.

Benton, are you okay?

It was noon, and he still wasn't home.

I paced the apartment, too erratic to sit still or take a nap to pass the time. The house was dead silent because I didn't have the TV on. The quiet felt like surround sound I could actually hear.

Benton?

He told me to only call for emergencies and text for everything else. But I was tempted to make the call, just to know that he was okay, that he would be home in an hour or two. The wait was agonizing, and I realized I couldn't do this forever. I couldn't wait up for him every morning, wondering if he was still alive.

He texted me back. *Baby, I'll be home in fifteen minutes.*

The gasp I released was so loud it sounded more like a scream. "Oh, thank god…"

In exactly fifteen minutes, he came home, and I

could tell he was in a bad mood. It wasn't just the blood on his shirt—but the look in his eyes.

"Are you hurt?" I rushed to him, my hands flattening on his stomach.

He pushed my hands away. "It's not mine." He headed straight for the kitchen and raided the fridge. He pulled out the plate I'd made for him and threw it in the microwave for a minute or two.

I just stood there and waited for an explanation.

He didn't seem to be in the mood to talk because he wouldn't even look at me.

He leaned against the counter with his arms crossed over his chest, the microwave lit up as it heated his food. The next few minutes went by that way, and I assumed he was too hungry for conversation, so I let it stay quiet.

When his food was ready, he took it to the table and scarfed it down.

I got him a glass of scotch before I sat across from him.

With his eyes down on his food, he ate, shoveling bites into his mouth and gulping it down like he was starving.

He probably hadn't eaten since dinner last night—and it was almost one.

When he finished everything, he took a drink, and finally, the tension left his face.

I'd never lived with a man before, but I quickly learned not to bother with conversation if he was hungry. Once he was full, he was a different person, far less intimidating.

He looked at me for the first time.

"I'm sorry you had a rough night."

"I'm done with Bartholomew. Once I find us a place, we can go."

"What…? He just let you go?"

"He didn't *let* me do anything. I left."

"What about Forneus? Could we kill him instead?"

"You know if that were an option, it would have been my first choice."

"Why isn't it your first choice?" I wanted him to pay for all the emotional distress he caused, for killing those innocent people at the market, for the deaths of all the women who came before me.

"Because I can't take down him and all those freaks and protect you two at the same time. I'm sorry, I know that's not what you wanted. It's not what I wanted either. The safety of my family is more important than my need for revenge."

I forced myself to give a nod. "I feel like there's something you aren't telling me…"

He stared for a long time, his blue eyes a shield against his soul. "Because you can read me when no one else can."

"What is it?"

He sucked in a slow, deep breath before he began. "Everything that's happened…it wasn't by chance. Bartholomew made some mistakes after I left, and once he realized he couldn't overcome them on his own, he knew he needed me back. So, he did whatever was necessary to make that happen."

My eyes shifted back and forth, not understanding the tale.

"He arranged everything."

"As in…he abducted your daughter so you'd need him to get her back?"

He shook his head. "It was supposed to be just Beatrice."

"I…I can't believe this."

"Forneus is a loose cannon, so he couldn't control him. Then I made everything more complicated with you. Now I understand why he said everything he said…because saving you sabotaged his entire scheme."

I continued to shake my head. "I still… Do you think he's lying? Do you think he did mean to take Claire?"

"No."

"Are you sure?"

"Beatrice would have sufficed."

My eyes glanced down to his stomach, which was blocked by the table. "Did you kill him?"

"Not sure. But whether he lives or dies…told him to stay the fuck away from me."

"How could he do this? I thought…I thought you were close."

All he did was stare.

"I just don't understand how he could do something like this if he ever cared for you."

"It's…complicated."

"I don't think it's complicated at all."

"We live in a different world…express ourselves

differently. Different rules apply to us. And he…doesn't have the cognitive ability to understand my feelings for Claire. It's hard to explain."

I needed a few seconds to process what he said. "Correct me if I'm wrong here…but it almost sounds like you're sticking up for him…for putting your daughter through hell."

"Incorrect. I just understand who he is, how he thinks, the context. You have no grasp of the context because you don't live in that world. He wanted me back and was willing to do anything to make that happen—not realizing he'd made a deal with the devil. But in the end, it doesn't matter. We're leaving all of this behind to start new lives in a beautiful place. Canada has the highest quality of life out of all the countries in the world, so it's a great place for us to start over. I'll do construction again. You can dance if you want. Claire will make friends. Everything will be as it should be."

I wanted to bash Bartholomew's face in with a bat for the suffering he'd caused Benton and Claire, but Benton was right. It was done now. Time to move on with our lives. Move on to better things. "Okay."

―――

I PICKED up Claire from school while Benton slept at home.

Christmas had been a month ago, and we were about to break into February, another cold month. I'd wanted to spend the summer at their estate in the countryside, but that wasn't going to happen. Canada was a pretty cold place…so I guess I'd better get used to it.

"Constance?"

"Yes, honey?"

She walked beside me, her backpack bopping up and down as she worked to keep my stride. "I have to tell you something…"

"What is it?" I kept getting distracted in my daydreams, thinking about that conversation with Benton, that Claire ended up at the cult because Bartholomew decided it. If I weren't there to protect her…what would have happened? All that blood would have been on Bartholomew's hands. The scars on Beatrice's back…they were carved by Bartholomew.

"I broke my promise."

"What promise?"

She gripped the straps of her backpack as she kept her head down. "When you told me not to tell Daddy what you said about him…"

I jogged my memory as I tried to think of the incident she referred to. Then it dawned on me. "You told him I loved him?"

She closed her eyes in a cringe. "Sorry…"

"Why? Did he ask?"

"No."

I released a sigh. "Then why did you do it?"

"I don't know… Because I want you guys to get married and live happily ever after."

It was sweet enough to warm my heart, but I was

still thoroughly embarrassed. "What did he say when you told him?"

"Nothing."

Of course he did. He'd already said he didn't love me. Geez, this would be awkward.

"I asked him if he loved you too, but he said that was between you guys."

I didn't know how I would face him. Would he be distant? Would he avoid me? "Claire, when did this happen?"

"I don't know…a couple days ago."

"Oh…" Nothing was different between us, so I guess it didn't bother him after all.

"I'm really sorry. I just got so excited…"

My arm moved around her shoulders, and I brought her close for a hug. "It's okay, honey. But if someone makes a promise, they should keep it. If you don't keep it, other people won't trust you to keep the promises you make to them."

"That's what my Daddy said too."

"Then let's learn from this."

———

HE WAS UP AT DINNERTIME, as if he could smell it through the crack at the bottom of the door. He was in his sweatpants, but this time, he wore a shirt, hiding those ripped muscles under a blanket of cotton. He went for Claire first, enveloping her in his fatherly affection.

I watched him run his fingers through her hair and listen to her go on and on about school, about what Angelica said at recess, the art they were making for class, and all the nuances of her little life. Sometimes it didn't seem like he even listened to her but got lost in a daze instead, looking at her bright little eyes with a sheen of unconditional love.

I loved it when he looked like that—wore his heart on his sleeve.

When their conversation was finished, he joined me in the kitchen and took a peek at the pans on the stove. All it took was a single glance at the food for him to turn into a chef and add more salt and pepper, along with the other spices on the counter. He even changed the heat setting on the pans.

I crossed my arms over my chest and leaned against the counter.

The corner of his mouth rose in a guilty smile.

"You don't like my cooking?"

He walked over to me, his big arms swaying slightly with his gait, and pressed right up against me at the counter. His head bent down so our eyes could look into each other. "I love your cooking, baby." He gave me a soft kiss, PG on the surface but smoldering hot underneath, then stepped away.

He turned around and grabbed the dinner plates from the cabinet.

I admired his muscled back, the sharp cuts between the muscles, the tight skin over masses of power, all visible through the fabric of his shirt whenever he moved.

Once I knew Claire had broken her promise, I'd started to tread water. My stomach tightened in discomfort, and I felt a flush of anxiety in my chest. I was a bit embarrassed, too, because I knew my feelings weren't reciprocated. But he wasn't distant or appearing to be uncomfortable. He was exactly the same—as if my feelings were irrelevant.

Any other man wouldn't have reacted that way. They would have gotten uptight and quiet. Would have pushed me away. Would have looked at me differently. But this man was…not like the others.

―――

BENTON WANTED to do Claire's nightly ritual of getting her ready for bed and tucking her in. He was in a noticeably better mood, always wearing a slight smirk on his lips, and he looked at his daughter like she'd just been born.

I knew the source of his happiness.

He didn't have to go back to the Chasseurs.

He could stay home with us every night forever.

I cleaned up the kitchen and did the dishes before I sat on the couch with a glass of wine.

He emerged from the hallway a moment later, a shine still in his eyes.

"Eh-hem."

His eyes narrowed as he halted in front of the fireplace.

I made a gesture with my fingers, telling him to take his shirt off.

When he understood, he gave a grin and pulled it over his head.

"Thank you."

He tossed it on the armchair then knelt in front of the fireplace to put another log on.

I sipped my wine and enjoyed the view. All the muscles shifted and moved with his actions, a symmetrical collage of mobile strength. He got to his feet once more, then joined me on the couch. The bottle of wine was on the coffee table, so he helped himself to a glass and took a big drink.

He didn't drink wine like a wine drinker.

He inhaled it like everything else.

He got comfortable beside me, his arm moving over the back of the couch behind my neck, his knees opening far apart. His blue eyes watched the fire burn in front of us.

I watched him, my hand on his thigh. "What about Bleu?"

"What about him?"

"Will he come with us?"

He shrugged. "That's up to him."

"Have you told him yet?"

He shook his head. "Haven't had a chance. I'll start looking for a place tomorrow."

"No rush."

He turned his head to regard me.

"Now that you'll be home, there's not much he can do at this point."

"I'm still ready to move on."

"Yeah…me too. I feel guilty for leaving those girls behind, but I don't know how I can help."

"Don't feel guilty." He watched the fire again. "You wouldn't want them to feel guilty, right?"

I shook my head.

His fingers moved to the back of my head and lightly played with my hair.

My hand tightened on his thigh. "Claire told me she told you…"

His fingers went slack.

I stopped breathing, and that was when I noticed my heart pounding harder and harder.

"I told her it's important to keep the secrets someone entrusts to her. That loyalty is more important than anything else. I hope she'll learn from this—and I hope you aren't angry with her."

"Angry?" My voice cracked with a smile. "No…I could never be angry with her." Impossible.

He looked at the fire again.

"That…doesn't bother you?" I didn't know what I was hoping for by digging. He'd already told me how he felt. If that had changed in the last month, he probably would have said it.

"Why would it bother me?" He turned back to me, looked me square in the eye.

My heart gave a quick jolt when I felt the rays of his confidence, of his power.

He continued the stare, his gaze intense, unyielding.

I would suffer the same fate a million times… because it brought me here. It brought me to this man—the only man I'd ever loved. Now that I knew how it felt, this profound explosion inside my heart, I knew why it'd never happened before. Because loving somebody the way I loved him…was rare. You didn't meet in a bar and then skip off to happily ever after. You didn't share a few laughs in a café then fall into this deep of a connection. Our relationship was born of mutual suffering, terror, and love. No one else understood it except the two of us.

Now I was on my knees between his, my fingers scooping into his waistband so I could drag his pants down to his knees.

His eyes took me in for a moment, darkening in intensity, and then he lifted his hips so I could get them down. His big dick landed against his stomach, and every time I looked at it, it seemed to be hard, like he was always ready at a moment's notice. I never had to get him ready, never had to set the mood to get him to play.

I scooted myself between his open knees and started with a kiss against his balls.

Both of his arms moved over the back of the couch as he got comfortable—and he let out a quiet moan.

My tongue glided around and wet the skin, feeling it tighten with pleasurable contractions the longer I kissed him. Like they were marbles, I pulled them into my mouth and swiped my tongue across the textured grooves of his body.

His breaths increased, growing deeper, more labored.

I dragged my tongue up his base, traced it over the thick veins right on the shaft, and then made it to his thick head. My lips surrounded him, and I gave him a soft kiss before I flattened my tongue and pushed him inside me.

He gave another moan, this time louder.

When I got going, moving up and down, pushing him deep into my throat until I couldn't breathe, his hand gripped the back of my neck, and he guided me at the pace he wanted. His breathing grew deeper and harsher, moans escaping in between, and he thrust a little harder as the minutes went by.

Tears dripped from my eyes and I struggled to breathe, but I kept going, my panties soaked because of the way he visibly enjoyed it. There was nowhere else I'd rather be than on my knees between his, worshiping this man for being the god that he was.

EIGHTEEN

Benton

CONSTANCE WAS ALWAYS UP FIRST THING IN THE morning, making breakfast and taking Claire to school, so I turned off her alarm before it could go off and handled it myself. It'd been so long since I'd had this luxury, to wake up and take Claire to school like old times.

I made her favorite—mushroom crepes with ratatouille.

When she was ready to go, we walked out together, the crisp winter air immediately dry against the skin. My breath came out like vapor, like I had a cigar in my mouth and a cloud of smoke in my lungs. I used to smoke all the time, but once Claire came, I quit cold turkey. Wasn't even hard.

"Why didn't Constance come with us?"

"I wanted her to sleep in."

"I don't think she wants to sleep in. She likes taking me to school."

I smiled. "I know she does, sweetheart." We stopped at the corner and waited for the light to change. Claire knew when it was about to, so she took a step before it was officially green.

I snatched her by the arm and tugged her back. "Always wait until it's green."

"But it was going to change—"

"Doesn't matter. You wait. Understand me?"

She nodded.

We crossed the street and made it to her school. Parents dropped off their kids, and just like old times, the moms all looked at me the second I was on campus. I wasn't involved in school functions, except for parent-teacher conferences, but everything else I avoided. Wasn't my thing. And didn't want these single mothers taking their shot.

I gave Claire a hug and a kiss on the forehead before I said goodbye.

She ran off right away, headed straight to a group of her friends outside the door to their classroom. They all smiled when she came, genuinely happy to see her. She must have said something funny because they laughed a moment later.

Sometimes I would just watch her, see the way she interacted with other kids, the way she was different from when it was just the two of us. She had her own life outside of the house, her own experiences, something I wasn't a part of.

That was how it should be.

The Catacombs

I had Constance now—and she was my own experience.

I turned away and left campus, crossed the street that Claire had tried to rush, and then halted when I saw him.

Leaned up against the building with his arms crossed over his chest, it was Bartholomew. It was like seeing a vampire in daylight—something that shouldn't be possible. Dressed in all black with his military boots, he was exactly as I remembered. And he wore that empty look, his gaze impenetrable.

I held his gaze.

"I'm alive, but you don't look too happy about it."

I turned away and kept walking.

He followed me. "Benton."

"I said I never want to see you again." I halted then turned around. "What part of that didn't you understand?"

His eyes narrowed as they focused on my face, his look dark despite the sunlight heavy on his cheeks. "The part where you called Ian to tell him I needed help right after you left."

I kept my face hard as stone.

"Benton—"

"I'm not coming back."

"Not why I'm here."

"I don't care why you're here. Leave me the fuck alone." Other people passed on the sidewalk as they headed to work and school, and they didn't seem to notice the two of us in a verbal battle.

"You know me. I don't make apologies—"

"And you know I don't accept them."

He slid his hands into the pockets of his jacket. "I accept your resignation, Benton. But I don't accept your withdrawal."

"Withdrawal from what?"

He stared at me for a long time before he made a slight gesture between us. "Us."

I gave a loud sigh as I looked away.

"I would never put Claire in jeopardy—and you know that."

"You had ample opportunity to get her back—"

"I had no fucking idea that they took her until you came to me. And once I knew, you bet your ass I tried to get her back before I got a damn thing from you. But it was too late. Forneus took off running."

With a clenched jaw, I shook my head. "You saw what they did to Beatrice—"

"I had no idea—"

"Fuck off, Bartholomew. Don't play stupid when we both know you're the smartest motherfucker in this town. Don't act like you didn't know what you were doing as you were doing it. Maybe shit got out of hand, but you still orchestrated the beginning of this nightmare. All because you still held a grudge—after all these years."

He breathed heavily for a while, his eyes hard. "You're right. I never forget a slight—and you slighted me hard. But the betrayal was different from all the others, because this was fucking personal. I let my anger get the best of me, let it simmer these last seven years, and then I did something I shouldn't have done. Benton, I'm sorry. Fucking sorry. I'd take it back if I could—"

"But you can't. And I'm moving to Canada anyway, so…"

His shoulders fell the same way his eyes did.

I turned away before he could say anything back. "Goodbye, Bartholomew."

———

CONSTANCE WATCHED me move about the house, watched me grab the bottle of scotch and fill a glass even though it wasn't even noon. She watched me flop down on the couch in front of my laptop. "Something happen?"

I took a drink and kept my eyes focused on the screen.

She came closer. "What is it?"

"Nothing."

"Benton—"

"I said, nothing." This time, I looked up at her to drive the message home.

She held my gaze for a while before she returned to the bedroom. The door shut a moment later.

I turned back to the screen and continued my search for a new home. I'd never been there before, but

I had to find the right place with the right school system, a place where we'd be happy a long time.

I continued to drink and drink, and before I knew it, it was noon and my mind was foggy.

Constance took the decanter away and placed it inside one of the cabinets. "Enough of that…" She moved about the kitchen and made lunch, ignoring me all the while.

I eventually joined her and grabbed one of the pans.

She pushed my hand away. "I've got it."

I saw the way she wouldn't meet my gaze, the way she pretended I didn't exist. "You're mad at me."

"Yes."

"I'm not obligated to tell you everything—"

"When there's a psycho putting acid in my food and stalking me day and night, yes, you're obligated to tell me." She stared at me head on, a fire in her eyes. "I haven't seen you head straight to the bottle since we first met. It was like going back in time…"

"I'm sorry."

"Don't be sorry. Tell me what happened." Now lunch was forgotten, this conversation taking over the kitchen.

"Bartholomew."

"So, he survived?"

I nodded.

"What did he want?"

"To apologize—even though I'll never forgive him, regardless of how many times he apologizes."

"You aren't going back. He's wasting his time."

"That's not what he cares about."

"Then what?"

I gave a shrug.

"What, Benton?"

I leaned against the counter, my arms crossed over my chest. "As I said before…we were close."

"You didn't speak for seven years—and that didn't bother him then."

"He's stubborn."

"So stubborn that it took him seven years to do this when he could have just picked up the phone?"

"He knows I wouldn't have answered."

She stood in front of me, her arms crossed over her chest too. "You come in here pissed off like a bull, but when I ask you about it, every answer you give is calm and simple. So…why were you so angry in the first place?"

I stared at her face, seeing the way her eyes showed the depth of her intelligence. She constantly collected information, constantly surveyed the world around her with pinpoint accuracy. It was to my detriment sometimes. "I'm not sure."

"It sounds like you still care about him."

"It's…complicated."

"It's not too complicated for me to understand, Benton."

My eyes dropped to the black-and-white checkered tile beneath us. "I know how he thinks. I see him make bad decisions for the right reasons. I see him try to reconcile his logic and his emotion. This decision he made…was just like one of those. It was a bad decision, but he didn't know what else to do."

"He could have just talked to you."

"There was nothing he could have said that would have made me change my mind. It was the only way to get us back to where we were. It was a bad decision… for the right reasons. I know he's sorry. I know he wouldn't put Claire in jeopardy. That's why it's complicated."

HAIR WET with a towel around her body, she stood in front of the mirror and ran her fingers through the strands. The towel would slip sometimes, so she would tighten it and keep going, unaware of my stare in the bathroom mirror.

I could see her from where I lay on the bed, the light from the vanity giving her face a beautiful glow. Her face was free of makeup, but her green eyes still stood out like the lights on a Christmas tree. She was gorgeous with no effort. She didn't have to wear a short dress that barely covered her ass and do her makeup heavy to get a date at the bar. She was all natural—and all perfect.

I tossed my phone aside, dropped my sweatpants, and then moved behind her.

She instantly stilled when she saw my naked body

emerge behind her, my shoulders a foot higher than hers, my stare more intense than the sun.

My hand gripped the towel, and with a gentle tug, it fell to the floor.

Her skin was still a little wet, and her small tits had hardened nipples from the abrupt change in temperature. Her stomach tightened when I drew near, her breaths increased, her eyes hardened as she looked at my reflection.

My arms wrapped around her, one across her tits, the other across her stomach. I squeezed her tightly, my hard dick right against the small of her back. My head dipped, and my mouth closed around her neck, my eyes still on the mirror to see her reaction to me.

She sucked in a deep breath as she tilted her head, giving me plenty of access. Her arm moved around mine, her nails lightly clawing me like a cat that enjoyed a good pet. She even purred for me with her pants.

I continued to kiss her as I tugged her into me, wanting her as tight against my skin as possible.

"Benton?"

I kissed her shoulder on the top, my eyes on the mirror.

She held my look as she grasped on to me. "I want to have more children…"

I stilled as I held her against me, felt her heart pound a little harder against her flesh in anticipation of my answer. "Alright." My lips dipped back to her shoulder, and I gave her hard kisses. "Now?"

"You'd…want them now?"

"I want what you want." I turned her around then lifted her onto the counter so I could take her on the edge. My hand guided my dick past the tightness of her entrance, immediately smothered in her arousal. "So, if you want me to knock you up, tell me. Because I'll do it."

NINETEEN

Constance

With Claire gone all day, it was just the two of us. We had lunch together, screwed on the couch, talked in front of the fire, had the solitude we never really had before. We fell into a routine right away, and then it felt like it'd always been that way.

I started to feel like Claire was mine even though I knew she wasn't. I had memories of being pregnant, of giving birth, all of which were hallucinations. Beatrice could have had this life but chose not to. I chose to have it.

"What do you think about this place?" Benton turned the laptop toward me.

It was a large house on several acres of land, surrounded by tall pine trees, had a private gate. It was much too big for three people, so he'd taken what I had said about more kids seriously. "What about your horses?"

"It'd be too much work to move them. I know a couple places that will take them."

"Will we get more horses?"

He turned to me. "Do you want more horses?"

"I think Claire would."

He turned back to the screen. "I guess I'll have the free time to do that…"

"But it's beautiful."

"It's a ten-minute drive to school and town, both of which are great."

"Sounds good to me."

He handed the laptop to me. "Take a look and let me know."

I clicked through the pages, seeing a beautiful fireplace in the living room, a kitchen much bigger than the one he had now, and plenty of bedrooms for a couple more children. I also noticed the price tag and did a double take.

He made himself an espresso in the kitchen then looked out the window as he drank it.

"I like it."

"Alright." As if the matter was settled, he returned to the couch and grabbed the laptop again. "I'll get it done."

"Do you like it?"

"I picked it out, didn't I?" He grabbed his phone.

I checked the time. "I should go pick up Claire. Are you coming?"

"I've got to get the ball rolling on this."

The Catacombs

"Alright." Before I left the couch, I planted a quick kiss on his lips.

His arms circled me and pulled me close, making something that should have lasted just a second stretch into several.

Not that I minded. "I'll see you soon."

I CROSSED the street and reached campus, passing parents who had gotten there before me. They went to their cars parked on the street or walked to their nearby apartment just the way I did. Some kids lingered on the benches and stone planter boxes, their backpacks beside them.

If I wasn't there before the bell rang, Claire usually waited on the bench near the road, but she wasn't there today.

I headed closer to her classroom, knowing she must have gotten caught up talking to one of her friends somewhere. But when I got there, she wasn't there either. The door to the classroom was open, so I stepped inside, expecting her to be talking to her teacher at the front of the class.

But she wasn't there.

Now I started to panic. "Mrs. Kyte, have you seen Claire?"

She looked up from her desk. "She walked out with Angelica when the bell rang. Are you having trouble finding her?"

"Yes…"

"Let me call the security guard. I'm sure he can help."

"Yeah…thank you." I walked back outside and scanned left and right, searching for the pink backpack with ponies. Now my heart was a hammer in my chest, and I could barely get a breath into my lungs. "Claire? Claire!" I started to run—even though I had nowhere to go.

I went to the principal's office and then the bathroom, anywhere I thought she could be. "Claire!"

Then I halted when I saw them.

Across the street on the corners…the Malevolent.

Skulls with antlers hid their faces. They were the only ones there…because they'd scared all the other pedestrians away. They were sprinkled along other streets, extending at least half a mile away, only distinguishable because of their appearance.

That was when I knew. "No…"

With shaky hands, I fumbled for my phone, dropped it once, and then finally called Benton.

He answered right away. "Baby, I'm on the other line—"

"He to-took—Cl-Claire." I could barely get the words out because the sobs drowned out my voice. I couldn't even see, the tears were so bad. Pain flooded my brain, emotional pain that was so physical it felt like my body was on fire. "She's go-one."

TWENTY

Benton

The rifles and handguns were dropped on the table, and I strapped on my bulletproof vest. The front door opened, and in tears, Constance stepped inside, her hands clutching her arms as she proceeded to break down right in front of me.

I couldn't help her right now.

"What…what are you going to do—"

"I'm going to kill every motherfucker in that place and get my daughter back."

She approached the table, picked up a rifle, and tried to make sense of it.

"You're not coming with me—"

"I'm coming…" She forced a deep breath and steadied her tears as best she could. "That's final. Get me one of those vests and show me how to use this thing."

The front door opened again.

I pushed Constance out of the way and fired the second I saw his face.

Bartholomew ducked and barely missed the bullet. He righted himself a moment later, brushed off the dust from his jacket, and then stepped into the room. "I need to speak to you in private—"

"They took Claire! I don't have time for your bullshit, Bartholomew."

He glanced at Constance before he looked at me again. "That's why I'm here."

I was too angry to think straight. The second Constance called me, my vision had tinted red, and all I wanted was to kill every motherfucker associated with Forneus. I would burn that place to the ground and everyone in it.

Constance silently excused herself, her cries echoing all the way down the hallway, even when the bedroom door was closed.

I stared at Bartholomew, so livid that a migraine immediately appeared at my temple. My broken heart was working so hard, harder than it ever had, and it strained every vessel and joint.

Once Constance was gone, his hard expression fell, revealing the softer side of him I barely saw. He came closer and kept his voice low even though Constance couldn't hear a word. "He wants a trade. Claire for Constance."

"You knew about this—"

"He called me after it had already happened. He said she's in a room with a TV and some toys, completely unharmed. She's asking when you're going to come get her."

The rage dwindled, and some of the tears I'd been fighting came through.

There wasn't a hint of judgment in his eyes. "I don't think you have a choice here, Benton."

"We could kill him instead."

"I have no idea where he is, and even if I could hunt him down, you're putting Claire at risk."

I closed my eyes, more tears coming at just the thought.

His hand went to my shoulder. "I'm sorry."

I shoved his hand away as I collapsed in the chair. The room started to spin. My heart turned inside out, and the blood seeped deep into my chest cavity. The pain was so raw, so potent, that I could barely handle it. I felt my body grow weak, like it wanted to stop working just to spare me the pain. Like death was the only solution that my mind could handle right now.

He pulled up a chair and sat right across from me, the guns on the surface between us. He stared for a long time, waiting for me to speak whenever I was ready to. When nothing came, he spoke again. "He said once the trade is made, you'll never have any kind of interaction with him again. You and Claire can live your lives without fear. If you try to take Constance back…then he'll kill Claire."

I inhaled a sharp breath, the kind that made my eyes water in a different way. I felt so much rage but had nowhere for it to go. I felt so much sorrow that my heart couldn't contain it any longer.

At least ten minutes passed, and nothing was said. Helpless, all I could think about was my daughter trapped in a room, waiting for me to come get her. I'd come for her last time—and she knew I would come again. But it came at a price…a price so heavy that it was like a Clydesdale standing on my chest.

He rose to his feet. "I'll get the time and place…and let you know."

"We do this now." My eyes dropped to the table, thinking about my little girl surrounded by those freaks. Whenever she was scared, she crawled underneath furniture and pulled her knees to her chest. I knew she was doing that now—and it broke my heart. "I'm not…I'm not leaving her there for a second longer than I have to."

CONSTANCE HAD STOPPED CRYING.

While her eyes were red and her cheeks puffy, the rest of her skin was pale white, like the snow we rarely had in Paris. She sat beside me, the fire in the hearth so dead that the coals weren't even red anymore. All she did was breathe in and out—each one deep and purposeful.

We were quiet for a long time, neither one of us able to speak to the other. That morning, it was a regular day. We had breakfast, took Claire took to school together, and then spent the rest of the day in each other's company.

But that dream was shattered when we lost Claire.

Now there was nothing but frost between us.

Constance was the first one to break the silence. "What's the plan?" She gave a loud sniff before she wiped her nose with her wrist.

The words didn't come to me.

"What did Bartholomew say?"

I stared at my hands clutched tightly together, my phone sitting on the table with a dark screen. I waited for it to ring, waited for the appointment to be made. "Baby." I wanted my daughter back to the exclusion of everything else, so the choice was simple, but that didn't make it hurt any less. It didn't make me feel less barbaric, less disloyal. I didn't just have one girl—but two. And I was throwing one to the wolves to protect the other. "Forneus will return Claire…in exchange for you."

The deep breaths stopped.

The silence was so profound it was as loud as a scream.

There was no point in holding back. It needed to be done—quick and painless. "I've agreed." I forced myself to raise my chin and look her in the eye, to face this decision like a man.

Instead of being full of despair, her eyes relaxed, like this was the sign of hope she'd been looking for. "When?"

I hesitated because I'd expected a different reaction. "Tonight."

She gave a firm nod as her hands clasped together. "Okay."

Her participation didn't make this better. Only worse. "I'm sorry—"

"Don't be. As long as Claire is safe…I don't care."

The next breath I took hurt so fucking much. "He said if I try to get you back…he'll kill Claire."

She nodded, as if she was prepared for that. "I'll be fine, Benton." She turned to stone, her face expressionless, her body motionless. There were no tears. No sign of fear. She took her sentence like a man.

"I'm going to get you back." My heart ached as I stared at her because she was my whole world, exactly as Claire was.

She slowly turned to regard me, her eyes pained. "You just said they would kill Claire if you tried—"

"How can they kill Claire if they're all dead?"

"Benton, no." She pivoted on the couch, so she faced me head on. "It's not worth the risk. I don't want you to do it."

"Baby, I can't just leave you there—"

"You're going to because I'd rather die there than risk something happening to her. You know I'm right."

I'd been through a lot of tough shit, like when Claire was taken from me for months and I had no idea where she was. But this was harder, being faced with this horrible decision. The longer I dragged it out, the longer Claire was locked up, and the harder it became for me to even think straight. It was like a hand had a grip on my heart, constricting so hard that it couldn't beat.

"You know you can't. I wouldn't want you to."

I dropped my gaze, feeling worthless in that moment.

Her hand reached for mine, and she squeezed it—comforting me when I should be comforting her. "I always knew I was on borrowed time. I always knew this freedom was short-lived. I always knew I would end up back there…"

I couldn't look at her.

"But this time with you and Claire…has been the greatest time of my life."

I lifted my chin and looked at her once more, and it hurt so fucking much.

"I'm grateful that I got to have it."

My fingers squeezed hers back, feeling that gentle and steady pulse under my fingertips. I wanted to treasure what little time we had left. I wanted to take her into the bedroom and enjoy her before I had to let her go. But my heart was somewhere else. I couldn't focus on anything knowing my daughter was unsafe, so I really couldn't cherish these final moments with Constance at all. I wanted her to leave as soon as possible—as terrible as that sounded.

My phone rang on the table, and I answered it within the first second. "What's happening?"

"He's ready whenever you are."

I couldn't look at Constance. Just couldn't do it.

Constance must have heard because she said, "We're on our way."

Bartholomew heard her. "I'll pick you up in ten minutes."

CONSTANCE SAT in the middle of the back seat with Bartholomew on the other side of her. Her gaze was straight ahead, bags under her eyes like she hadn't slept in days when this nightmare had only gone on for a couple hours.

No one said anything.

Bartholomew kept his gaze out the side window like he wanted to give us whatever privacy he could spare.

I wanted to comfort Constance, but I couldn't do that when I counted down the streets until we reached the Louvre. I wanted to burst out of the car and sprint the rest of the way just to get there faster. The streetlights lit the way, cars passing the opposite way of us. It wasn't as late as it normally was when we'd met up, but I couldn't wait that long.

A moment later, we pulled up to the Louvre.

Bartholomew hopped out of the car first, along with the driver.

That left the two of us.

I looked at her, at a complete loss for words.

"Let's go," she whispered. "I'm just as anxious as you are."

We got out, and like I had twice in the past, I

walked up the stairs and approached the glass pyramid that stood erect. A few people were there in the plaza, but once they saw the skulls and antlers of the Malevolent, they ran for their lives.

Once I had a full view of Forneus and his men, my eyes scanned for my little girl with her long blond hair, her beautiful blue eyes, the outfit she'd worn to school that morning. But she was nowhere to be found. "Where is she?"

It was as if Forneus hadn't heard me because all he could do was stare at Constance. His eyes widened and exposed more of the white parts of his eyes than I'd ever seen before. He was still, and then slowly, his lips pulled back to show the most terrifying smile I'd ever seen.

I couldn't believe I was about to let this happen.

But I didn't have any other choice. "Where's my daughter?" I stepped in front of Constance, blocking her from Forneus's view.

Once she was invisible, the smile faded. His eyes shifted to me, angry.

Now I raised my voice, screamed the way Forneus had screamed when I'd denied him his heart's desire. "Where the fuck is she?"

He looked over his shoulder and gestured to one of his men.

My hands tightened into fists and gripped the air so I wouldn't grip my gun instead. My ribs ached from all the deep breaths I took, the way they expanded and contracted to make room for my desperate lungs. Everything hurt. Everything.

A moment later, two Malevolent appeared, Claire between them.

She looked exactly as she had that morning, with a pink bow in her hair, the straps of her pink backpack still over her shoulders. Her eyes were down on the ground, doing exactly what Constance had told her to do—not look.

I didn't think twice before I moved forward and crossed the distance between us so I could grab her.

"Wait." Forneus placed his hand on her shoulder and halted her.

"Don't you fucking touch her…"

When she recognized my voice, her eyes lifted. "Daddy?"

My eyes started to smart, but I didn't let the tears escape. My eyes stayed on Forneus. "I'm here, sweetheart. We're going home, okay?"

Her voice came out as a whisper. "Okay…"

Forneus nodded to Constance. "You go first."

My breaths grew deeper, harder. There was nothing I could do but hand her over and hope for the best. "Cross me, and you're dead."

Forneus only stared at Constance now. "Your daughter means nothing to me. I have what I want. My an-gel."

A boulder dropped into a pool of acid in my stomach.

"An-gel, co-me he-re." His unblinking stare never left her face.

I didn't have to ask her to do it. Constance made the move on her own, coming to my side. Before she crossed no-man's-land to Forneus, she turned to me, her eyes pained and her smile fake.

"I'm sorry." It was all I could say. Words that wouldn't change anything.

"I know." Her arms circled me, and she hugged me —one last time.

My arms latched on to her, and I squeezed, my chin resting on her head, feeling her and smelling her during our final embrace.

She rested her forehead against my chest as she stood there, her heartbeat so gentle and quiet, so calm. She spoke words against my chest, just loud enough for me to hear. "I love you." Then she raised her chin and kissed me on the mouth. It was a soft and short kiss. It wasn't warm like it used to be. It was just there, nothing like it could have been if the situation had been different, if I were dropping her off at the airport for a trip or something else. Then she let me go—and she was gone.

The goodbye was such a shock to my system that words left me. I couldn't do anything other than watch her walk away.

With his gaze on Constance, Forneus lifted his hand from Claire's shoulder.

I snapped out of it once my daughter was free. "Claire." I kneeled and watched her run to me as fast as she could, as desperate to land in my arms as I was to hold her in them. She hit my chest, and I scooped her up right away, my body throbbing now that I had her back. I felt the tears burn my eyes as I clutched her to me, my heart healed now that she was safe, that she was with me again.

But then I had to watch Constance.

Forneus stared at her, his eyes taking in all of her features, committing them to memory, treasuring them. The stare was intense, possessive, raw. He came closer to her, getting a deeper look into her eyes.

She held her ground and didn't blink.

I had to stand there and let it happen.

Forneus reached for her hand and interlocked their fingers.

She didn't pull away—but a momentary look of disgust crept into her eyes.

"Come on, An-gel." He guided her away, and the Malevolent closed around them, obscuring them from view.

I knew that I would never see her again.

And that hurt—so fucking much.

TWENTY-ONE

Constance

He didn't drug or blindfold me.

There was no point.

Benton wouldn't come to my rescue, and without him, there was no escape from that place. Even if I tried to run, I wouldn't get far, and if he caught me again, I wouldn't be surprised if Forneus threatened to hurt Claire if I tried to flee again.

We took a chopper just the way Benton had, and when we landed next to the trees, they were caked in snow. It was February now, the end of winter, and hopefully spring would bring a new beauty to this place.

Maybe I could learn to appreciate it.

If I wanted to survive, I had to convince Forneus I was the real deal, that I truly was a fallen angel, walking among mortals.

But did I want to survive?

Not really.

Not anymore.

Without Benton and Claire, my spirit was officially broken.

We walked through the tree line and saw the cabins scattered among the trees and statues. It was exactly as I'd left it, still and quiet, covered with a blanket of Malevolent that peered through the eye sockets of their skulls.

Home sweet home.

Instead of taking me back to my old cabin, he escorted me up the hill to his, past the church that he used as a confessional. The Malevolent were everywhere, and there seemed to be more than before.

He stepped inside his cabin, where a fire was already burning in anticipation of his arrival.

The door was shut, and we were alone, but my heart didn't race like it used to. I was totally numb, unable to feel fear or anything else, not even stress. Once you didn't care if you lived or died, you were granted overwhelming peace. That was how I felt now. Whether he gave me a piece of paper, a pill, or just wanted to talk, it made no difference.

Claire was safe. That was all I cared about.

He took a seat in the armchair, his eyes looking me over like it was the first time he'd seen me, like he couldn't believe I was real.

I took a seat too, finally comfortable in a chair because I didn't have those bulky wings behind me anymore. The costume had been warm, though. Now I was in just a blouse and jeans, and that didn't protect me from the cold. Not the way Benton's body did. Not the way his fireplace did. Not the way the love in my heart did.

With his elbows on his knees, Forneus stared, his eyes steady and locked on my face.

We spent the next thirty minutes that way, him enjoying his prize.

I looked at the fire, forgetting he was there most of the time.

One thing did hurt. I'd told Benton I loved him… and he didn't say it back. I wished we'd been together a little longer because perhaps he would have said it then, would have made my sacrifice a little easier. But maybe it was better that he didn't. Maybe it would be easier for him to move on…and forget about me.

"I missed you, An-gel."

My eyes shifted back to Forneus.

"I've worshiped you in your absence. I never forgot you—not for a single day."

I figured.

"Now that you're with your demon again, everything will be as it should be."

Maybe in a few months, maybe in a few years, I would end up in that graveyard too. A blank tombstone would stick out of the dirt. When the cult was over and someone new moved in, they would find the bones, but I would never be identified. My body would be far too decayed by then—as if I'd never existed at all. "I'm sorry that my absence has taken such a toll on you. I'm here now—for whatever you need." It was so easy to lie, to play the character he wanted, because I didn't care anymore.

Slowly, his face pulled back in his ridiculous smile. He showed all his teeth, every single one, somehow making his jaw move in ways it shouldn't.

I was totally unaffected by it at that point. "Tell me your sins, Forneus. Let me absolve them so we can ascend."

I WAS BACK in my old cabin—and I wasn't alone.

I had a new roommate.

With dark brown hair and blue eyes like crystals, she was beautiful. Her skin was the color of snow, her lips the color of a rose. And she was young, younger than I was by a few years.

I introduced myself. "Constance."

"Rayna." She shook my hand. "I'm sure you have a lot of questions—"

"Nope. Not my first time."

Her eyebrows furrowed as she looked at me.

"I was here a couple months ago. Got away…but my demon came for me."

"I…I'm so sorry."

"Yeah, pretty shitty."

Her eyes fell, like she'd just lost all hope.

"I'm sorry too. You don't deserve to be here. Nobody does."

"I just got here a couple weeks ago…"

"Who's your demon?"

"Amon."

Fuck.

"Yours?"

"Forneus."

"I think I've seen him before…he's the one with the smile."

"Yep, that's my man."

She released a chuckle—a very painful one. "I just had dinner. There are some leftovers on my tray if you're hungry."

I shook my head. "I'm good. Not much of an appetite." I bet Benton was making Claire's favorite tonight—mac and cheese. She'd probably asked about me, tried to understand what happened earlier that evening, and I had no idea how Benton would answer. "I think I'm going to get some sleep."

"Alright, goodnight."

"Goodnight, Rayna." I changed into my white linen pajamas, looked at the golden harp by my bedside, and then got under the sheets. The door between our rooms was closed, and then the moonlight came through the windows. I stared at the ceiling, the cabin cold and my body heat not enough to keep me warm. I wasn't used to being alone. I was used to having a man at my side, his powerful arms around my body, his quiet breaths my lullaby.

I felt a couple tears fall from my eyes to my ears, but I didn't wipe them away.

Just let them fall.

WHEN I LEFT my cabin the next morning, I came face-to-face with someone I hadn't seen in a long time.

Rebecca.

"You're still here?" I walked past her, my bare feet on the cold stones over the grass since they'd taken my shoes again.

"I need to speak with you for a moment."

I whirled around. "Still not an angel, huh? They didn't promote you when I was gone?"

Her face drained of color.

"Consider yourself lucky. Unless you're a Victoria's Secret angel, it's not worth it." I moved forward without looking back, and this time, she didn't follow me. I went up the hill toward the church, moving through the sea of Malevolent that watched my progression. "Long time no see, huh?" I approached the graveyard and noticed there were more graves than before. Three more.

Selfishly, I hoped it was no one I knew.

I entered the church and noticed that the windows were still covered with the paper I'd taped to the surface in another lifetime. A few angels were there, all dressed in their ridiculous gowns and heavy wings. Some of them looked at me, women I didn't recognize, but there was one woman I knew.

Laura.

She slowly got to her feet in sheer disbelief. "Constance…"

"I'm back, bitches." I raised my arms in mock celebration. "Couldn't stay away, you know." I walked up to her and embraced her with a strong hug. "How are you holding up?"

She pulled away, still in shock. "Let's skip the small talk, alright? What the hell are you doing here? We thought you escaped."

"I did." I took a seat and crossed my legs. "But I was never really free. I was still imprisoned, just in a different place. Forneus was always around, always looking for a way to take me back."

"You didn't go to the police?"

I told her that hadn't gone anywhere and that there was no real way to ever be free.

"Then how did you stay out for so long?"

"Claire's father, Benton."

Her eyes narrowed.

"He protected me…for a while. But then Forneus took Claire, and he didn't have a choice but to make the exchange."

Even though she'd been trapped this entire time, she still managed to have some pity for me. "I'm sorry."

"I'm happy that Claire is free. I'm happy that this will officially be behind her. She can live a normal life now. I always knew I was on borrowed time. I was always running from him, even when I was still. He was creeping up behind me, getting closer and closer. It was more like a vacation…a very short vacation."

"What's your plan now?"

"Plan?" I asked.

"You want to do the boats again? Spring is coming, so the snow will melt. The rivers will be full, and we won't freeze to death."

I shook my head.

"Then what's your idea?"

"I don't have one."

Her eyes shifted back and forth.

"You were right, Laura. There's no way out of this place. Just gotta make the best of it…"

———

I STOPPED for a moment to look at the moon.

It was full, luminescent, powerful.

All my surroundings shook as if there was an earthquake. Trees swayed left and right. The ground trembled beneath my feet. The starry sky spun in a circle, and the only thing that remained was the moon.

My heart raced harder than it ever had before. My brain thudded with a migraine. But I kept myself calm…at least I tried. The moon was my north star. The moon was real—but everything else wasn't.

"An-gel."

I heard his voice but didn't look.

"Look at me."

I tore my gaze away and met his eyes.

They were black. They were the same. But everything else had changed. Horns protruded from his skull. Sharp fangs hung from his jaw. His face was bigger than it used to be, more grotesque, with a smile so big and so sinister.

This isn't real, I told myself over and over again.

"Let us ascend."

His hand reached out for me, his claws digging into my flesh.

It's not real.

I did my best to erase the demon, to erase the hallucination, to calm my heart before I collapsed. The only thing I could picture was blue eyes in a different face, short blond hair, a hard jawline that was soft when it wanted to be.

Benton formed in front of me, strong and proud, looking at me like it was just the two of us. "This is real."

"This is real…"

TWENTY-TWO

Benton

CLAIRE WASN'T THE SAME.

Not because she was scared or traumatized.

But because Constance was gone.

Days passed, and I took her to school every morning, picked her up afterward, just like old times, but it didn't feel like old times at all. A piece of us was missing. Our family was fractured.

Claire used to be all I needed, but now I was incomplete.

I couldn't sleep. I'd lie there thinking about Constance, worried about her, drowning in self-loathing for allowing it to happen. I didn't put up a fight because I couldn't. I had to sacrifice one girl for the others, and that choice couldn't change.

But I still felt like shit anyway.

We sat together at the dining table. We ate the dinner I'd made, grilled chicken in a light sauce with rice and vegetables.

Claire chose to play with her food instead of eating it.

I didn't give a damn anymore, so I let her do whatever she wanted.

"Daddy—"

"No."

She looked up at me, her face scrunching up like she would burst into tears. "You can't just leave her there!"

"Claire."

"No!" She slammed her fist onto the table, and I'd never seen her do anything like that. "She took care of me, Daddy. We're supposed to take care of her. You said we were a family—"

"And I meant that."

Now she started to cry. "Then we have to go get her—"

"Sweetheart, you don't understand." I wouldn't tell her about the threat Forneus made. I wouldn't scare my little girl with that information. I'd just have to swallow it and look like the bad guy.

"I thought you cared about her…"

It took all my strength not to let my eyes water because she didn't understand all the turmoil in my heart every second of the day. "I do…very much."

"What if that was me, Dad? What if I was stuck there—"

"Nothing would stop me from getting to you—"

"Then why not her?" she asked through her tears. "I'm family…so is she."

"Claire, stop it."

"No!" She grabbed her plate and threw it on the floor.

The shatter was so loud, and then it was engulfed by the silence. The sheer silence.

I didn't move, because I couldn't believe that had happened. Claire had never acted out that way—not once.

She stormed off and ran to her room.

The door slammed a second later.

I didn't go after her. I didn't clean up the mess. I just sat there.

I just sat there because there was nothing I could do.

———

WHEN CLAIRE WAS AT SCHOOL, it was just me at the house.

I stopped working out. I didn't start up the construction company again. Honestly, I just sat on the couch and drank.

My nights were restless because she wasn't there, and her clothes and her smell…just tormented me. My mind always shifted to her, wondering what she was doing at the camp, if she was high on acid, if she was even alive.

I used to be the one thing she trusted to keep her safe.

But I was the one who handed her back.

If she'd resisted, I would have drugged her,

restrained her, done anything necessary to hand her back to Forneus. Fortunately, she made it easy on me, walked right up to him without being forced. Claire was everything to me, and I would sacrifice anyone in a heartbeat for her. I knew that made me a monster.

A fucking monster.

Now my daughter thought I was a monster too.

I sat there with my scotch and watched the fire burn. I didn't know how to move on from this. I didn't know how to get up and walk away. How did we go back to our normal lives like nothing happened, when we both knew exactly what Constance suffered?

The front door opened.

I stayed on the couch and didn't rise. I didn't expect company, and I knew Forneus would keep his word now that he had Constance, so that could only leave one person.

He rounded the corner, dressed in his jacket and black boots.

I held his gaze for a moment before I turned back to the fire—and kept drinking.

Bartholomew lowered himself into the armchair a moment later then helped himself to a drink. An extra glass was there, so he filled it halfway then got comfortable, one boot against the edge of the coffee table.

He was so quiet I forgot he was there after a couple minutes.

"Benton."

My eyes left the fire and moved to his face instead.

"Doing alright?"

I took a drink.

"How's Claire?"

"What do you want, Bartholomew?" My glass became empty, and I left it on the cushion beside me, a single cube still at the bottom. I had to cut myself off because I couldn't be a drunk instead of a father.

"To see how you're doing."

"How I'm doing…" I gave a subtle nod. "My daughter hates me because I won't get her back, and the only woman who's ever meant a damn thing to me is in hell…and there's nothing I can do about it. That's how I'm doing."

He set his glass aside and sat there.

I went back to ignoring him.

"Benton."

I gave an angry sigh before I looked at him. "If you think sitting here is making me feel better, you're wrong. Nothing will make me feel better. Now, piss off."

His face was as hard as the foundation homes were built on. "Let's get her back."

My eyes narrowed.

"We can do it."

"What the fuck are you saying?"

His eyes remained still, unblinking, emotionless. "I'm saying, let's go to the godforsaken camp and get your woman back. Let's kill that freak. Let's kill all the freaks. Let's set it on fire so the forest smells like burning flesh. That's what I'm saying, Benton."

Now I took his words with a grain of salt. "You'll do anything to get me to come back…"

He gave a subtle shake of his head. "You don't owe me anything, Benton."

"I'm not stupid."

"You are. Because I just offered this to you freely, and you still won't take it."

"Nothing is free when it comes to you. If you think I'm going to feel indebted to you and return of my own free will, you'll be disappointed."

"That's not what I expect. That's not what I want."

"Then what do you want? Because you don't do anything out of the goodness of your heart. There's always an angle. There's always a reason. Tell me what it is."

He looked away for a while, his gaze on the fire. "Your friendship…that's what it is."

I stared at the side of his face.

"If you let me redeem myself, then maybe there's a chance." When I didn't say anything, he turned back to me, his gaze still cold as if his heart wasn't in the conversation, as if he didn't just put himself out there to be rejected once again.

"I can't risk Claire."

"Ask Bleu to take her away. Not to tell a soul where he's going. When it's safe for him to return, we'll leave a message on the answering service. He'll call and check in every day, and when he hears that message, he knows it's safe to return. We'll keep this between the three of us so there are no leaks."

"Is this just you and me? Or is this the Chasseurs?"

"It's whatever you want, Benton. We can discuss the logistics."

"You'd be declaring war—which you said you wanted to avoid at all costs."

He shook his head. "It's not war. It's an annihilation. Big difference."

My daughter was my soul, and I didn't want to risk her, not for anything. And I didn't want to risk myself either because that would mean she'd grow up without me, that she wouldn't have me to protect her.

But I had to get my woman back.

"Why didn't you tell her?" he asked.

"Tell who what?"

"When you said goodbye. She said she loved you, and you didn't say it back."

I held his gaze, surprised he'd heard her whisper that to me.

He waited for an answer.

"'I love you' and 'Goodbye' should never be in the same sentence—at least, not the first time you say it."

"I KNOW it's a lot to ask."

Bleu sat across from me at the dining table, Claire in her room because she took off the second she finished eating. She wanted nothing to do with me, could barely tolerate me being in the same room with her. I had a seven-year-old last week, but now I had an angry teenager instead.

It was hard, but I didn't let it bother me. It was temporary, and I understood why she was upset. She missed Constance, and that feeling had manifested into anger. She was just like me—because I did the same thing.

Bartholomew sat on the opposite side of the table, nursing his glass in silence. It was one of the few times I all three of us were in the same room.

Bleu held his silence for a long time. "It is a lot to ask, Benton."

"But you're all I have. I need you to do this for me."

"You're asking me to raise your daughter if you don't make it back. You're asking me to stay behind when I should watch your back for this. I'm supposed to just take off…without looking back?"

"Bleu, the only reason I can do this is because I know my daughter will be safe. You're the only man I trust for the job. If I don't make it…I know you'll raise her how I want her to be raised. I know you'll love her like she's your own."

He dropped his gaze.

"Bleu."

"What if I take your place, and you run off with Claire?"

I shook my head. "It needs to be me."

"Why?"

"Because she's my woman." Nothing was going to stop me. Bullets. Knives. Fire. Nothing. "And I have a lot more experience than you do. Taking Claire to safety is not cowardly. This entire operation depends on you—because you have the most important job."

He raised his gaze again.

"You're the only person I trust to do it."

After a long stare, he gave a nod. "When?"

"Now."

He stilled. "You want me to do this *now*?"

"Yes. We want to make sure you're far away before we make our move."

"When is this happening?"

"The second we get the plan together—and not a moment later. The longer she's there…" The less likely it was that she was still alive. Forneus didn't go through so much trouble just to kill her, but I wouldn't be surprised if he gave her too much acid on accident, and then she would be gone.

"Alright," Bleu said. "I'll think of a place."

"And somewhere far away, Bleu. Far."

He nodded.

Bartholomew pulled the papers out of his pocket. "These will get you anywhere you need to go. Pay for everything with cash. Leave your phone behind and take this instead." He pulled out a phone and tossed it on the table. "Call the number every day. We'll leave a message when it's safe to come back."

Bleu looked at the cash and papers then looked at me again. "You better come back, alright?"

I nodded.

"Not just for her—but for me too."

SHE DIDN'T HAVE A SUITCASE, so I packed one of mine.

Clothes, shoes, her bows, and most of her stuffed animals. Coloring books, colored markers, stickers, stuff that would keep her busy so Bleu wouldn't lose his mind trying to keep her entertained. She had a couple books she liked, but that was her least favorite hobby. She was like me—liked to do things with her hands.

When it was done, I zipped up the suitcase and set it on the floor.

"Daddy?" Her quiet voice came from the doorway to her bedroom. While I'd packed, she'd visited with Bleu, being a lot warmer to him than she'd been to me all week.

I didn't look at her. "What is it, sweetheart?"

"What are you doing?"

I kept my eyes on the suitcase.

"I'm sorry…please don't go." She immediately burst into tears. "Please don't leave me. I'm sorry, okay?" She sprinted into me on the floor and latched on, like the ground disappeared beneath her feet. Her little chest pressed against me every time she gasped for breath. "I won't do it again."

"Claire—"

"You're leaving me like Mom…"

My heart was glass, and she threw a brick, shattering it. I almost called the whole thing off. "Sweetheart." I pulled her away from me so I could see her heartbroken face. "I'll never leave you. Don't ever think that, okay?"

"You promise…"

I nodded. "Cross my heart…hope to die…"

"Stick a finger in my eye?"

I nodded again.

"Then what are you doing?"

I remained kneeling on the floor as I rubbed her arms, our eyes level. She was tall for her age, but I was enormous compared to her, so taking a knee was the only way I could make her feel equal. "I'm getting Constance back."

Her eyes immediately lit up. "You are?"

She looked at the suitcase. "I'm coming too?"

"No. You're going to go on a little trip with Uncle Bleu until I get back."

"Oh…"

"It'll just be a couple days."

Her eyes fell, and she looked devastated all over again.

"Sweetheart?"

"I'm scared."

"There's nothing to be scared of—"

"It's a really scary place, Dad. I…I don't want you to be scared."

Her heart was so pure, I couldn't believe it. Far purer than mine. "Daddy doesn't get scared."

"Everyone gets scared."

Losing my girls was the only thing that frightened me to my bones. "I don't."

"Constance must be so scared…"

I shook my head. "Was she scared when you were there?"

She shook her head.

"She's okay, Claire. But she's going to be more okay when I bring her back."

She gave a nod. "I still…I still don't want you to leave."

"I know, sweetheart. You have no idea how hard it is for me to leave you. Just dropping you off at school in the mornings breaks my heart. I wait all day until you come home so I can hear about your day. But we both need to be brave—because we need to get Constance back where she belongs."

Her lips trembled for a moment before she gave a nod.

"You'll be good for Uncle Bleu?"

She nodded.

"Good." My arm circled her and brought her into me. Her head dipped onto my shoulder as her arms wrapped around my neck. I held her there as I resisted the tears in the backs of my eyes. I'd never cried in my life—until I had my daughter. Now the tears were easy to provoke. All she had to do was say she loved me, that she missed me, that she didn't want me to go…and I was a puddle on the floor. "I love you, sweetheart."

"I love you too, Daddy."

TWENTY-THREE

Benton

I STOOD ON THE SIDEWALK AND WATCHED THE taillights glow in the dark. Bleu pulled away from the curb and drove off, moving farther and farther from where I stood. My eyes stayed on the truck until it turned to the right—and then it was gone.

Claire was gone.

Bartholomew came to my side, and the second my daughter was gone, he lit up a cigar and let the smoke rise to the cold sky. "I'll give you some time."

"I don't need time." I turned back to the apartment. "Let's get to work."

Bartholomew followed me back inside the silent apartment, the sounds of Claire's absence as loud as a trumpet, and the depression sank a bit deeper. It reminded me of those terrible months when she was gone, when I feared that it would only be me from now on.

I grabbed the scotch and fell into a chair at the dining table.

He joined me.

I gave a loud sigh. "How are we going to do this?"

"We only have two options." He held the cigar between his fingertips as his elbow rested on the table. "We hit them with everything that we've got. Or we sneak in—just a couple of us."

"If we hit them hard, they'll see us a mile away."

Bartholomew nodded. "I know they have scouts in cabins farther away from the camp, so they'll report us before we get there. I know they've got a stockpile of weapons at their disposal, some serious shit."

"How do you know this?"

"I talked to their arms dealer. Got the inventory."

"RPGs?"

He sucked on his cigar as he gave a nod. "Could shoot down our choppers before we even land. If we take the Hummers, it'll be more of the same. We can let the men go first and we pull up in the rear, so they'll die instead of us."

"And if we sneak in?"

"Horses."

Neither plan was great. A couple men weren't enough to overthrow that camp, but if we came with guns blazing, they'd shoot us out of the sky like clay pigeons. "What should we choose?"

"Do we know where they keep their weapons?"

I shook my head. Even if I could ask Constance, I doubt she'd know.

"Do you know where her cabin is?"

I shook my head again.

"We could do surveillance for a while. Live in the woods."

"I suppose."

"Neither is a good decision. Because if we get caught on our own, we stand no chance to get away."

True. "We could start a fire along the edges of the camp."

"We have no idea which way that fire will go. Might go the wrong direction."

Fuck. "I remember Constance saying something about a church…"

He took a drag of his cigar as he stared at me.

"It's the only place where the women go that they can't be followed. The windows are covered."

"What are you thinking?"

"We get in there and give them weapons. There've got to be at least twelve. They can hide the guns under their gowns."

"And then what?"

"They can kill their demons. Those are the guys we need to worry about—not the Malevolent."

He considered the idea before he gave a slight nod. "I'm sure they won't miss—because they've got to be pissed."

"I'll handle Forneus myself."

"I think your girl deserves that honor."

"If he knows it's over, he'll kill her. And I know that's a battle she can't possibly win."

He gave a slight nod. "No dibs in my book. I'm going to kill every motherfucker that I see."

WE DROVE the trailer down vacant country roads until the roads ended. It was just an endless tree line with the mountains in the distance. Snow covered the trees. A thin line of mist rose into the sky, the cold air almost visible to the naked eye.

Bartholomew gazed at it. "Would be a lot more beautiful if it wasn't cold as shit." He hopped out and moved to the trailer.

I joined him, my bulletproof vest strapped underneath my long-sleeved shirt, and opened the door in the back to get the horses.

Bartholomew already had a cigar in his mouth. "The men are ready. I just have to call it in, and they'll arrive in ten minutes."

"Alright." I guided my horse by the reins and tied her up against the trailer. She was a mare I'd had for years, a horse Claire had affectionately named Princess. I rubbed her behind the ear then gave her a pat on the flank.

Bartholomew got his horse ready and tied another to his rear. We needed an additional horse to carry all the extra supplies, mainly guns. He climbed on top of his horse and waited for me to do the same. Then he pulled out a cigar, lit it, and handed it to me.

"You know I don't smoke anymore."

"Well, this might be your last chance." He continued to hold it out.

I took it and popped it into my mouth before I kicked the horse.

"Just like old times…minus the horses."

———

IT TOOK us an entire day to approach the camp. Bartholomew used his phone for direction, having pinned the location of the camp on his maps app. There was no designated path to get there, except one.

It was visibly marked by tire tracks, especially in the places where the snow was the heaviest.

That was the main path they used to bring supplies to the camp, so we steered clear of that and took the path less traveled. Deep inside the trees, the snow was higher because it was colder under the shade of the branches than out in the open. But the horses continued to move, and we only stopped once or twice so they could eat and drink.

At nightfall, we arrived.

Torches were slightly visible through the trees. They were small and unnoticeable to most people, but not to us.

I was so close to Constance now, and it was hard not to grab my rifle and run straight to her.

We tied up the horses and went the rest of the way on foot. When we had a good view of the camp, we kneeled and surveyed the activity. In the light of the torches, it truly looked like a place that didn't belong on the surface of this planet. Sculptures of demons were in the center of the pathways, some nine feet tall, some so small they were hard to make out. The Malevolent were everywhere, scattered throughout the grounds, not speaking to one another, just existing.

Bartholomew gave a shake of his head. "Freaks, man…"

I noticed a woman emerge into my vision, carrying a tray of food. She wasn't one of the girls because she wasn't dressed in white. She didn't wear wings. That meant she was one of them. And it sickened me that a woman would participate in this foul place. She opened the door to a cabin, went inside, and then returned a moment later.

"Dinnertime."

My eyes moved up the hill to the other buildings. It was hard to see because there were few torches that high, but I could see a building that looked distinct from the others. It was white, made of birch, and it didn't look like a cabin. "That must be the church."

Bartholomew followed my gaze. "You're probably right. You see that other one?"

"Where?"

"To the right. You can't miss it."

I turned my gaze the other way, seeing a building made of black rock, with no windows.

"I don't want to know what the fuck goes on in there." Bartholomew stepped away and returned to the horses.

The Catacombs

I followed him. "We'll go around the rear so we can get closer to the church."

"Yeah, that's what I'm thinking."

"BENTON, YOU SHOULD SLEEP." Bartholomew spoke from his bedroll on the ground.

"Someone's gotta keep watch."

"None of those freaks are going to come over here. Trust me."

I continued to sit up against the tree.

"You won't be doing anyone any favors if you're exhausted tomorrow."

I gave a sigh before I lay in my bedroll beside him. We were both on our backs, side by side, straight on the ground after we'd cleared away the snow. It was a clear night, so I could see the stars between the silhouettes of the trees. "I want to kill him now."

"I know."

"No, you don't know. You have no idea…"

AT FIRST LIGHT, we moved for the church.

The Malevolent hadn't swarmed it yet, so that was our opportunity to slip inside unnoticed. Claire told me they pressed their faces against the windows when the women were inside, so that meant they followed them wherever they went.

There were rows of seats and an altar at the front. Statues of angels were dispersed around the room. A chandelier hung from the wooden beams in the ceiling. My skin immediately prickled once I stepped foot inside.

Bartholomew gave a quiet whistle. "And you think I'm the crazy one…" He set the case of rifles on one of the seats and dropped down next to it, immediately stretching out to get comfortable. "My back hasn't been this stiff since Positano."

"I don't want to know."

He gave a smirk.

I took a seat across the aisle and waited.

Waited for Constance to walk through that door.

I wasn't sure how much time passed. An hour. Maybe two. Maybe an eternity. It definitely felt like an eternity.

Finally, the door opened.

I got to my feet, imagining her long brown hair and her green eyes. But the morning light was too bright, and I couldn't distinguish anything, not until the door shut. When it did, everything came into focus.

Two women stood there, both brunettes.

But neither one of them was Constance.

They halted as they stared, as if they didn't know what to make of me.

I didn't know what to make of them either.

The older, lighter-haired brunette came closer. "Uh…who are you?" They stuck to the opposite wall, unsure if I was friend or foe.

The disappointment was almost too much to bear. "Benton." I nodded behind me. "Bartholomew."

Their eyes switched back and forth between us.

"Benton…?" the woman said the name slowly, savoring it. "You're not…Constance's Benton, are you?"

I swallowed, touched that she even wanted to say my name after what I did. "Yeah."

She came closer. "You're here to save us."

"Yes."

Now the younger woman came closer too, just as stunning as the taller woman, her hair a darker, richer shade of brown. They were both in the white gowns with wings, their hair curled, their makeup heavy. There was a strict dress code here, apparently. "What do you want us to do?"

"Get all the girls here."

"Some of them want to be here," the older woman said. "They actually buy in to this bullshit. I'm Laura, by the way."

"Rayna," the shorter woman said.

"Get them here anyway," I said. "We'll tie them up and keep them out of our way."

"Alright," Laura said. "We'll round everyone up." They both left the church in a hurry.

I took a seat again, and Bartholomew hadn't moved at all.

I just had to wait a few more minutes—and I'd see her again.

THREE OF THE women really believed they were angels and they needed to help their demons ascend, otherwise, their sins would never be absolved. They were tied up at the front of the church, but that wasn't enough for Bartholomew.

He taped their mouths shut. "Not gonna listen to this bullshit all day." He tossed the tape back into the bag and took his seat.

The women sat in a circle together, their backs against one another, their wrists all tied to the statue at the altar. All they could release were a couple muffled words, so they eventually gave up and turned quiet.

Rayna hadn't returned—and Constance wasn't here.

I started to get nervous.

What if I was too late?

The door opened again, and Rayna returned.

But she was alone.

No. "Where is she?" I stepped forward, my chest cracking in fear.

Rayna rushed over and joined us near the altar. "She's not in our cabin…so she must be with Forneus."

TWENTY-FOUR

Constance

I sat on the birch throne across from him, and just like old times, we sat there for a lifetime and didn't speak. His hands curled over the armrests as he sat there, naked from the waist up, built like a brick house.

He must spend all his time lifting weights and doing acid.

"What are your sins?" I finally asked.

His stare hadn't left my face, not for the last thirty minutes. He could stare at me forever, utterly fascinated by my appearance. His obsession was so deep, but not once had he tried to be physical with me. Perhaps my angel status made me off-limits in that way. I was too innocent, too pure.

Thank god.

"I have many."

Yeah, I figured. "I know you killed those people at the market."

"It was nec-ess-ss-sary."

Nope. "Still a sin."

"I did it for my an-gel. I had to."

Now he'd killed in my name, and that made me feel worse.

I thought I could play along to stay alive, but I wasn't sure if I wanted to be alive anymore. All those people died because of me. And then every day would be like this, listening to a maniac confess all his murders. We would take the acid, I'd hallucinate and feel like shit, and then I would do it all over again in a couple days.

What was the point?

There wasn't one. "Let's ascend."

He was always the one to initiate it, and he seemed slightly surprised that I took the lead. But he didn't hesitate to produce the paper and add the drop to the surface. He was about to place it in his mouth, but I stopped him.

"More."

He stilled at my words.

"We can't ascend with that." It was an out-of-body experience, a complete disregard for my life. I just didn't care anymore. I had no hesitation at all. This was how it was going to end at some point anyway. May as well just get it over with. "We need more."

He added more to the paper then handed it to me.

"More."

"An-gel."

I didn't press again, not when he used that tone. I

took the paper, popped it into my mouth, and hoped it would be enough to get me where I wanted to go.

We sat there together for a while, staring at each other, and slowly, my heart started to pick up the pace. It was a slow start, a jog that turned to a run, and then turned into a sprint. Just enough would send me into cardiac arrest. It'd been over within seconds, not enough time for me to even feel pain.

My vision started to blur. My surroundings started to shake. Forneus began to change.

And then I heard it.

Gunshots.

Or at least I thought they were gunshots.

The demon seemed to notice it too because his head turned to the double doors of the black church.

It was all in my head. It was part of the hallucination. I'd seen things that weren't real. I'd felt things that weren't real. But I'd never heard gunshots, especially not ones so loud they made me flinch each time.

The horned demon left his chair, his long tail behind him, spikes all over his body, even his back. He opened a door and grabbed something, something with a handle, a weapon of some kind.

Then he walked out.

The gunshots grew louder.

I gripped the armrests as I felt my body shake. It was the tremors from the acid, or it was just the fear that surrounded me. I'd never crashed this hard, never put myself in a nonexistent war zone.

I grew restless, unable to sit and wait for it to pass.

I had to move. Always had to move. Especially when the monsters crawled out of the shadows in the corners. I made it to my feet and stumbled to the door.

My body hit it, but it wasn't a door anymore. It was a mountain, a solid mountain I couldn't climb.

They were all behind me, snarling, their claws reaching for me.

"Not real…" I pushed against the wall, knowing it was the door, and found the handle.

The door swung forward, and I fell to the dirt.

The sunshine hit me hard in the face, and then the gunshots grew even louder. They came from all directions. The ground shook underneath me as I crawled forward, trying to flee the monsters that wanted to swallow me whole.

"Constance!"

I looked up, seeing the demon standing there with a sledgehammer.

And then I saw Benton…or at least I thought I did.

The demon gave a jerk and collapsed, the gunshot shattering my eardrum again.

"Baby." Benton rushed to me on the ground.

I kicked him as hard as I could and let out a scream. "Don't touch me!"

"Baby!" He grabbed me by the arms and forced me to still. "Look at me."

I kept trying to fight, uselessly. The gunshots kept going, and I gasped in fear every time I heard them. My body spasmed, and I convulsed in his grip.

"Shit." His arms scooped underneath me. "Baby, stay with me, alright? I need you to stay with me."

I saw him. The demon rose once again, his hand reaching for the sledgehammer. I tried to get the words out, but I was too slow. "He's coming…"

Benton didn't have ample time to react. He turned, but then the weapon came down on him, and then he was gone.

"Ahhh!" This was real. "Benton?"

No answer.

The demon looked down at me, nostrils flaring, his horns sharp and dripping with blood. "My an-gel." He turned away and raised the sledgehammer once again.

Come on, Constance.

My heart pounded as if it was about to explode, and my body wouldn't obey my mind. Every thought I had took forever for my body to follow. But a jolt of adrenaline hit me, a cloud of focus, and finally, the world stopped shaking. "Benton…" I dragged myself forward then crawled, crawled as fast as I could, and got on top of Benton's body.

It was all I could do.

"Move."

I looked up at Forneus. He wasn't the demon anymore. He was the man, with dark eyes that showed a glimpse of the underworld. There was a haze in the sky, but I could see the blue. I could see the clouds. I could actually see. And I could see the bullet wound in his chest, the stream of blood pouring out.

"An-gel. Move."

I swung my leg as hard as I could, kicking his leg from underneath him, his heavy body hitting the earth.

The sledgehammer dropped too...

Come on, move.

I left Benton and scrambled for it, but it was so heavy. I clenched my teeth and picked it up, but it was so cumbersome I couldn't even wield it. All I could do was keep it away from Forneus so he wouldn't smash Benton into pieces.

Forneus was back on his feet, his aggression on me now.

Good.

He walked toward me, my vision starting to transform him back into the demon.

No...gotta focus.

I did the best I could to defeat it, but it was a losing battle as more of the acid dropped into my bloodstream.

But if I didn't do this...Benton would die.

I gripped the handle. *You've got this, bitch.*

Forneus came closer and closer, his powerful arms rigid by his sides, horns on his head. Fangs protruded from his mouth, dripping with blood. He stared me down before he lunged at me.

I couldn't move with the sledgehammer, so I let it fall to get out of the way. I spun around, throwing my elbow wildly for anything that could cause injury. I hit him somewhere in the back, and my elbow immediately fired off in pain.

"An-gel." He spun back toward me and gave me a

The Catacombs

hard shove. "How dare you move against me? After everything I've done for you."

I scooted back, dragging my body over the dirt.

"You. Are. Mine." He picked up the sledgehammer along the way. "And your life is mine to take."

Shit.

He lifted the sledgehammer and prepared to slam it down on me.

Somehow, miraculously, I rolled out of the way.

The earth shook when the sledgehammer landed, like an earthquake had struck.

Another jolt of adrenaline hit me because I needed to take this opening. I needed to get to my feet and hit him from behind. A rock that could barely fit in my hand was on the ground, and I grabbed it in my fingertips before I rose up and slammed it into the back of his head.

He went down, face forward, and his palms caught him in the dirt.

I jumped on his back and slammed the rock down again, drawing a gush of blood from the back of his skull.

"Ahhh!" He threw me off, and with speed I couldn't replicate, he was on top of me, the bloody rock in his hand above my face. The obsession was gone from his eyes, and now there was just hate. Raw and unadulterated hatred.

I didn't know what else to do but shield my face with my hands.

Another gunshot rang out.

Forneus collapsed, the rock falling to the dirt.

My arms dropped, and I saw him beside me, his eyes still open in death. "Oh shit…" My attention immediately went to Benton, who was still on the ground, blood all over the side of his face and neck. In his hand was a smoking gun.

"Benton!" I crawled over, the world starting to shake again, the scenery blurring into shadows and monsters. My hand reached for his arm, and I swayed as I gripped him. "Are you okay…?"

"Baby, I'm fine." He pushed himself up with a grunt then pulled me close. His lips pressed against my forehead, and he held them there as we both breathed. "I need you to stay with me, alright?"

I nodded against him. "I took a lot…"

"I know." He got to his feet then pulled me to mine. He moved slower than usual, like he really was hurt. "Come on." He took my hand in his and guided the way forward. He pulled a radio out of his pocket and made the call. "Send the choppers."

TWENTY-FIVE

Benton

"Jesus fucking Christ." Bartholomew ran to me the second he saw me caked in blood. "What happened?"

"Sledgehammer."

He threw my arm over his shoulder to support me.

"No." I pulled away. "Constance…" I held her by the hand, lifting her up every time she started to collapse as the acid pulled her under. "We've got to get her out of here. She'll die if we don't."

Bartholomew abandoned me and went to her instead. He lifted her in his arms and carried her for me. "Come on, let's move."

The chopper landed in the field, and we ran across the grass to get there. The Malevolent had run into the surrounding trees, and the demons had been killed by the angels with their guns. Most of the cabins were on fire, but I didn't know who'd set them. Once the fight had broken out, I'd headed straight for the black church, ready to get rid of that fucker once and for all.

Now he was gone.

It was over.

Now we just had to survive.

Bartholomew got her into the chopper first and then came back for me. He gave me his hand and pulled me up to get me into my seat. He shut the door, and then we were off the ground. He started barking orders to the medic. "Pump her stomach. Now."

My mind started to go black. I did my best to resist, but the corners of my vision were fading.

"Benton, don't you fucking dare." Bartholomew struck me so hard I hit the wall. "Is Claire going to grow up without her father?"

I could barely get the word out. "No."

"Then get your shit together, or I'll punch you in the face."

The medic got to work on Constance on the floor of the chopper, putting her under before he stuck a tube down her throat to pump her stomach. It might be too late, but any bit that could be removed before it entered her bloodstream would make all the difference in the world.

Every ten minutes, I started to fade.

But Bartholomew was there to slap me hard.

"Thank you."

"I know you'd do it for me."

"With pleasure."

He grinned.

I grinned back.

WHEN WE MADE it to the hospital, we were pulled in separate ways.

I couldn't stay with her, and she couldn't stay with me.

I didn't know if I'd ever see her again—because one of us might die.

Didn't even get a chance to say goodbye.

I couldn't remember exactly what happened. I was seen by the doctors, they said something about surgery, and then I was under. The next time I woke up, I wasn't sure how much time had passed, but it must have been a while because Constance was at my bedside.

Her eyes watered as she looked at me, and her hand was in mine on the sheet.

"Are you okay?" The words barely came out, raspy like sandpaper.

"I'm fine."

"Am I…okay?" I felt the gauze on my head and was suddenly aware of the pain.

She nodded. "You had a skull fracture that was putting too much pressure on your brain. They repaired it. Said you'll be fine, that you don't have any serious head trauma. You're not going to lose your memory or have cognitive difficulties or anything like that…"

This felt like a dream, and I wasn't sure if it was real. "Bartholomew…"

"Right here." He came into my vision from the other side of the room. "You look like shit."

I never thought I'd be happy to see him again. "What happened?"

"Killed the twelve demons. All the Malevolent that were dumb enough to stay. The rest ran off into the woods, but they'll die out there anyway…so what does it matter. The girls were returned to Paris. Gave them some money to get home."

"That was awfully nice of you."

"You're paying me back for that, asshole."

I grinned.

He didn't grin back, but his eyes softened slightly. "The camp is gone. Nothing but ash and statues now."

"Fender said the same thing…then Forneus moved in."

"Well, let's make sure it actually stays that way this time."

"What about the acid?"

"I took that off his hands."

"Good. Now you won't need to knock on the Skull Kings' door."

He smiled. "Never said that was off the table."

I gave a sigh. "Your funeral."

"You'll give the eulogy?"

"Fuck off."

He grinned then stepped away. "I'll give you guys a minute. Something I gotta do anyway."

Once he was gone, my attention was back on Constance. We shared a long stare. My thumb brushed over her fingertips, and I appreciated the color in her face. She wasn't stark white and deathly. She was exactly as I remembered, with that small smile on her lips. "You saved my life."

She gave a little shake of her head. "You're the one who came back for me."

"I couldn't leave you there, baby."

Her eyes started to water more. "You shouldn't have…"

"You're my woman. I had to."

"Your woman?" she whispered.

I nodded. "The woman I love."

She drew a deep breath as her eyes started to water more, until they filled the brim and dripped over the edge.

"I promised you I'd take care of him."

Her hand squeezed mine, like she was at a loss for words.

"I'm sorry I let him take you in the first place—"

"You made the right decision."

"But I still felt like shit doing it."

"If it makes you feel any better…I would have done the same thing."

It did. "Yeah?"

"In a heartbeat."

She loved my daughter as much as I did—and that made me fall so damn hard.

"We're together now. That's all that matters."

"I worried about you—"

"It's over now. And I never want to think about it again."

I saw so much behind her eyes, so much that she wasn't telling me, but I let it go. "The last thing I remembered was you having a seizure. When I opened my eyes again, you were still going…somehow."

"Because I knew you'd die if I didn't."

"Then you knew I was real."

She nodded. "Whenever I see you…I know it's real."

I pulled on her arm. "Baby, come here." I tugged her onto the bed and against my chest, secure against my lips. I squeezed her as I kissed her, the pain in my head numb because her kisses were potent as medicine. Just like we were in bed at home, it was just us and the sheets, the rain against the window, our two broken souls healed together.

"Daddy!"

Constance pulled away when she heard my little girl.

I saw her at the doorway, my brother and Bartholomew behind her. She burst into tears when she saw me, all bandaged up in a hospital bed, and she ran to me as quickly as she could. She jumped on the bed and crawled into my arms.

I caught her, my chin resting on her head. "Sweetheart…I'm okay."

"You're hurt."

"Not anymore." I rubbed her back. "The doctors fixed me."

She pulled away. "But you have a thing around your head…and you're crying."

"I'm crying because I'm so happy to see you." I pulled her into me and kissed her on the forehead. "Really, I've never felt better."

I TUCKED CLAIRE INTO BED, gave her a kiss on the forehead, and then waited until she fell asleep before I left. When I returned to the living room, Constance was in the kitchen doing dishes, and a guest was at the dining table.

Bartholomew had helped himself to my scotch, and when I stepped into the room, he raised his glass before he took a drink.

I took a seat at the dining table. "Wasn't expecting company."

"And you should know that's exactly when to expect it."

"Bartholomew, the food's still warm," Constance said without looking at us. "If you'd like some."

He took another drink. "This is my dinner."

"Suit yourself." She continued to rinse and stack the dishes. "My cooking's pretty good…"

Bartholomew kept his eyes on me. "I'm sure it is."

Constance loaded the dishes in the dishwasher then came up behind me. Her arms wrapped around my neck, and she leaned down to give me a kiss on the cheek. Her fingers gave me a quick massage before she went into our bedroom and shut the door.

Bartholomew looked into his glass. "When will women learn we don't give a fuck about their cooking? We give a fuck about their fucking."

"I think I know why you're here."

"Good. So, you aren't going to make me say it."

I shook my head. "And you aren't going to make me give my answer."

His eyes darkened in disappointment. "The whole thing…made me miss the good ol' days. I thought you felt the same way."

"It's not as much fun when your family is the one on the line."

"Yeah, I get it."

"But I know what you mean…and I do miss it."

He held my gaze for a long time, his fingers around his glass.

"But this is my life now. There's no going back."

He nodded.

"I really hope you reconsider trifling with the Skull King."

"Come on, you know me better than that…"

"I thought everything that just happened would make you feel differently."

"Or make me want it more. Chaos—I live for it."

There was nothing I could say to change his mind. One day, he'd be dead, and I'd find out through an old friend.

"I accept your decision. I just hope that you can accept my friendship instead."

I shouldn't forgive him, not after everything that happened. But if none of it had happened…I wouldn't have Constance. I couldn't exactly regret that. She was the missing piece in my life. She was just like Claire. I didn't want her until I had her, and once I had her, I couldn't imagine a different way of life. I finally gave a nod.

Just the look alone told me how much that meant to him. "I'll get out of your hair." He rose to his feet and left his glass behind. "Until next time."

"Until next time."

I locked the door behind him then went into our bedroom. The lights were off like she was already in bed. But then I noticed her in the dark, wearing a sexy two-piece lingerie set made of lace. I stilled when I saw her because I'd never seen her dress up in anything like that before. It was just for me, and I enjoyed every inch of it.

She walked up to me, her hands working my jeans as she kissed my neck, getting the pants loose on my hips so she could pull everything down. I was a man who needed little foreplay to get ready, but she chose to caress me with kisses anyway, to let me know how much she wanted me when she didn't have to.

Her lips caught mine, and a few hot kisses ensued. Then she whispered to me, "I had my IUD removed today…"

My eyes focused on her lips as I processed what she'd said.

She moved farther away, so our eyes could lock on each other.

"You want me to knock you up, baby?"

She bit her bottom lip as she nodded.

"You want to marry me first?"

"A piece of paper doesn't make us family. We're already family."

"I don't think you understand what I just asked you."

Her eyes shifted back and forth as she looked into mine. "Did…you just ask me to marry you?"

I backed her up toward the bed. My shirt came off, and then I stepped out of my boots.

"Because if you did…you know what my answer is."

I got my jeans off then guided her onto the bed, dragging her until her head was on the pillow. "I want to hear your answer." I settled between her thighs and prodded inside her, giving a push against her entrance. I gave another thrust—and this time, I slid inside perfectly.

"Yes…" Her arms hooked around my neck. "My answer is yes."

Epilogue

CONSTANCE

I stood on the deck and closed my eyes.

The sunshine was so hot, burning my skin the second it hit my face. The day instantly warmed by several degrees when I stepped outside, feeling the summer heat I'd been craving all winter and spring.

Claire splashed the water with her hands. "Are you getting in?"

I opened my eyes and saw her in the water on a pink inner tube. It was a swan, and she could sit in it and kick around. "Is it warm?"

"It feels nice."

I grabbed the railing and moved down the steps, the water cool against my warm skin. When the water was to my chest, I felt the relief on my back now my weight had been lifted by the buoyancy. I went to her inner tube and spun her in circles, listening to her laugh as I made her dizzy.

When I finally gave her a break, she asked, "Where's Daddy?"

"Not sure. Might be working."

She stuck out her tongue. "Daddy sucks sometimes."

I laughed. "He does not suck."

She moved to the edge of the pool, which gave a breathtaking view of his property, the horses and ponies in the pasture as they fed on the fresh grass.

"Do you like it more here or at the apartment?"

"Here," she said immediately. "We don't have horses at the apartment."

I chuckled. "Yeah, that would be uncomfortable if we did."

"But when it's cold, there's not much as much to do here…so I don't know."

"I think I prefer the summer."

"Because we get to swim?"

"Yes, that's a big perk."

Benton finally stepped outside, in just his swim trunks and sunglasses, looking hotter than the underworld. "Got room in there?"

"Dad, take a swan." Claire kicked one toward the shallow end of the pool.

He stepped into the pool and then tucked the floaty under his arms as he came toward us. "Thanks, sweetheart. So, what were you girls talking about?"

"That we love to swim," Claire said.

"I noticed," he said. "You guys have been out here every single day."

"Yep." Claire dunked underwater then swam to the other side of the pool, to show off how long she could hold her breath under the water. When she reached the other side, she giggled. "Did you see?"

"I did," Benton said. "You're good, sweetheart."

"I can't wait until I have a brother or sister to swim with." She dipped below the water and did it again, swimming back and forth underwater, enjoying the praise she got from us every time she came up for air.

Benton stood next to me against the wall, his hand moving to my stomach under the water. "How's your back?"

"A lot better in the pool." I wasn't even that far along, but it was getting really uncomfortable—really fast.

"I know you can handle it, baby. And just remember, it'll all be worth it."

I watched Claire pop up for air on the other side of the pool, wearing her goggles. "I know. But then I've got to do it again…and again."

"Whoa, how many kids are we having?"

"I don't know. Guess we never really talked about it."

"You want to talk about it now?"

"Alright. How many do you want?"

He shrugged. "I guess if you ask me to knock you up, I won't have the strength to say no…so it's entirely up to you."

"Glad we had this conversation," I said with a chuckle.

He gave a slight smile, a handsome one. "Let's just focus on this one. We'll worry about the others later." He leaned in and kissed me, his hand still on my little stomach, a stomach that I could still hide under my clothes for the time being.

"That sounds like a good plan."

He pulled away and brushed his nose gently against mine. "I love you."

I melted every time he said that, like a stick of butter in a hot pan. "I know you do."

He turned toward Claire, who was on the other side of the pool. "You want to race, sweetheart?"

"Yeah!" Claire said. "Mom, you watch. And no cheating!"

My heart melted whenever she called me that, even though she did it every day now. Beatrice didn't want the title, but I took it with so much joy, the kind of joy that made my eyes water. Everything that happened was still in my nightmares, still ingrained in my blood, but I couldn't help but wonder if it was meant to happen.

Because if it hadn't…I wouldn't have ended up here.

Exactly where we all belonged.

New From This Author...

I'm taking a bit of a detour and trying something new… under a new pen name: Penelope Barsetti. You'll all recognize where Barsetti comes from and this new fantasy romance: ***Forsaken***

Readers have said, "It's got everything I love in her contemporary novels. Alpha. Feisty Heroine. Action. Betrayal. Pretty much everything!"

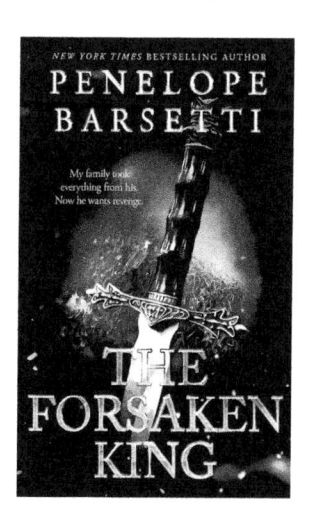

Ivory:

I see him watch me.

Everywhere I go—he follows.

He's one of my father's guards at the castle. Goes by the name Mastodon.

There's something about him I don't like, but my warnings are never taken seriously. But I bet if my brother voiced the same concerns that would be no issue…just because he has balls and I don't.

Well, I have bigger balls than he ever will.

When I leave for the Capital, Mastodon escorts me. And just as I feared, he kills my guards and captures me.

At least he tries to capture me. There's a lot of running and chasing. I land an arrow right in his neck, but it does nothing. It's like he doesn't even feel it.

He takes me into a cavern and we descend deep underground—to the Bottom of the Cliffs. Then he tells me why he's doing this.

Because my family took everything from him—and now he's about to do the same.

Mastodon:

Her father murdered mine then raped my mother—and forced me to watch.

Then he pushed us over the cliff—to our deaths.

But we survived—and now we're ready for revenge.

She's the key to that. After she helps us get what we need, I'll hang her by her pretty neck and watch her take her last breath.

I steal her from Delacroix—and of course, she fights me the whole way. Not just with her fists, but her mouth too.

If she wasn't my pawn, I might actually like her.

When I hand her over to my mother, I realize she has far more sinister plans. She tells me to do exactly what her father did—and force her.

That's not the kind of man I am, so the answer is no.

But then she asks Geralt—the most barbaric man I've ever met.

So I volunteer—because I know she'd rather it be me than anyone else.

<u>Order Now</u>